Roberta Latow has been an art dealer with galleries in Springfield, Massachusetts and New York City. She has also been an international interior designer in the USA, Europe, Africa and the Middle East, travelling extensively to acquire arts, artefacts and handicrafts. Her sense of adventure and her experiences on her travels have enriched her writing; her fascination with heroic men and women; how and why they create the lives they do for themselves; the romantic and erotic core within – all these themes are endlessly interesting to her, and form the subjects and backgrounds for her novels.

Praise for Roberta Latow's novels:

'A wonderful storyteller. Her descriptive style is second to none . . . astonishing sexual encounters . . . exotic places, so real you can almost feel the hot sun on your back . . . heroines we all wish we could be . . . irresistible' *Daily Express*

'The fun of Latow's books is that they are genuinely erotic . . . luxurious . . . full of fantasy. She has a better imagination than most' *The Sunday Times*

'Passion on a super-Richter scale . . . Roberta Latow's unique brand of erotic writing remains fresh and exciting' *Daily Telegraph*

'Latow's writing is vibrant and vital. Her descriptions emanate a confidence and boldness that is typical of her characters . . . you can't help but be swept along them. A pleasure to read' *Books* magazine

'Sex, culture an

'Intelligently w *Today*

G000139995

Her One Obsession

Roberta Latow

HEADLINE

First published in 1998
by HEADLINE BOOK PUBLISHING

First published in paperback in 1998
by HEADLINE BOOK PUBLISHING

10 9 8 7 6 5 4 3 2

ISBN 0 7472 5956 9

Printed and bound in Great Britain by
Clays ltd, St Ives plc

HEADLINE BOOK PUBLISHING
A division of Hodder Headline PLC
338 Euston Road
LONDON NW1 3BH

For Peter Dyne
in gratitude

To love him even more is erotic intensity,
corrupting sensual delight that rides on the wind.
A never-ending storm of obsessive love.

The Epic of Artimadon

FIRE ISLAND,
NEW YORK CITY

1993

Chapter 1

The house was quiet except for the sound of the electric mixer beating a batter for her pineapple upside-down cake. It was hot with not even a breeze to ease the stifling heat she loathed and Gideon adored. She wiped the perspiration from her forehead with the back of her hand and visualised her husband in his studio, naked save for a pair of navy blue swimming trunks. They were always navy blue, boxer-style, his Fire Island summer working costume. Gideon, his chunky muscular frame glistening with sweat as he worked feverishly on a painting, was still after thirty years the passion of her life.

She walked from the kitchen counter to the refrigerator, opened the pair of stainless steel doors and perused her morning's work: a clear glass bowl of creamy white potato soup with a sprinkling of snipped fresh chives; a platter proffering a mound of lobster chunks bound in her home-made mayonnaise, the orange-red claws already cracked and arranged round it; long, green asparagus dressed with her special vinaigrette; a plate of crispy cos lettuce, to be served with a Roquefort dressing, looking crisp and crunchy; ramekins of rich chocolate mousse and crème caramel. This was *her* work of art, all the things Gideon liked to eat, food she had mastered the making of to perfection.

She felt a sense of pride at what she saw, just imagining

Gideon's delight on opening the fridge and declaring what he wanted for his lunch excited her. Pleasing her husband was, after all, what she lived for. It was her excitement, satisfaction, somehow enormously erotic to her. She closed the fridge doors and returned to her mixer, checked the batter, and began laying pineapple rings in the bottom of the square baking tin.

The kitchen smelled of fresh-baked bread, cinnamon, cooking apples and sultanas from a pie she had made earlier. It was her domain, but not her only one. She was the mistress not only of the Fire Island compound but of a house on another island, Hydra in Greece, and besides that a three-floor loft space where Gideon worked and they lived, in SoHo, New York City.

Dendre Palenberg lived in three homes and two worlds: her husband's, and her own very private world of dreams and imaginings of how she would like Gideon to love her, rather than how he actually did. A fantasy to play with, nothing more. She had come to terms with that soon after they had met and married. How he loved her had not stopped her from loving him and the life he provided for her. She was a lady who knew how to live happily with compromise.

She heard the sea plane before she saw it coming in over the ocean. It circled the house once, twice: the signal that the passenger or passengers aboard expected to be met.

'Oh, damn,' she said aloud as she looked over the kitchen sink through the window. To herself she added, Where are the girls when I need them?

Gideon never met the plane. The children, if they had been there, might have, especially if the visitors were a mystery as these were. Who had Gideon asked for lunch and forgotten to tell her about? There was no surprise in that. It was rather the norm for him whose habit it was to extend a spontaneous invitation then forget all about it. A collector? A dealer? Some fun people to amuse him for a few hours? A pretty girl who inspired his lust enough to be a muse for him, at least for a while? His latest short-lived mistress? An artist friend of whom there were many? Yet another art historian? For certain it was not an art journalist or magazine editor. His dealer, Haver Savage, would have handled that and put Dendre on notice. That was about the only time the famous dealer ever communicated with her. Was it Haver himself?

Well, whoever it was, it was up to her to see that the plane was met. And that in the middle of assembling her pineapple upside down cake. What a nuisance! Especially so since she had fantasised all morning that she and Gideon might have lunch alone together. And that *was* a fantasy. They almost never had lunch alone together. Dining at the Palenbergs' Fire Island compound was always a plethora of food and people. There was the extended family to be considered: Gideon's three assistants and two handymen; Dendre's house staff of two – the indispensable Yukio, who acted as *major domo*, and Kitty the cleaner and cook who was rarely allowed in the kitchen; then there were the Palenbergs' three daughters, Daisy, Pieta and Amber. And one never knew who else would knock at the screen door and join the table. Usually if they dared they were welcome.

Gideon had been especially attentive when he'd awakened that morning. The sex they'd had together had been fiercely exciting for them both. Dendre could always tell what mood he was in by the manner in which he took command of their waking moments which happened most every time they slept together. This morning he had been happy, bursting with life and energy, powerful in his lust. He had told her as he sometimes did, in moments of passion, 'I will always love you more than any of the others.'

Dendre believed him. That was how she had survived years of his sexual peccadilloes. She could empathise with the other women's infatuation; she was herself still burning for Gideon, still a victim, as were they all, of his power as a man and a great artist; still ready to be seduced by his charismatic sensuality and his genius.

She was aware that she loved him obsessively and accepted that happily as *her* life. The way the art world laughed at her behind her back for being a dupe, for never having risen above her Brooklyn Jewish roots and being the kitchen drudge, the house-proud *frau*, meant nothing to her. She had the man they all wanted. It was *they* who had to toady to her to get to him, not the other way around. In the eyes of the world she was 'the painter's wife', the model for the many portraits that hung in prestigious museums and on the walls of collectors' homes in five continents. For that reason alone she was perceived as an important figure.

The plane buzzed the house one more time. That was unusual. Dendre turned off the mixer and snatched her daughter Daisy's sarong that had been left draped over the back of a kitchen chair. She wrapped it round her to cover herself and her one-piece black bathing suit, *her* daytime Fire Island wardrobe. From the rack at the back door she grabbed a battered wide-brimmed straw hat and slammed it carelessly on her head over the bright yellow scarf already covering her long, naturally curly, black hair. Stepping from the kitchen on to the wooden deck, she looked across the sprawling compound for someone. But it was quiet, with no sign of life anywhere.

She selected one of the small red wagons from a line of them under the deck and, taking hold of it by its long black metal handle, started across the sand to the boardwalk that led to the bay and the rickety wooden dock where their guests landed either by plane or boat. The wagon was for the luggage or any parcels that might be arriving on the plane.

Fire Island had no cars. People and goods arrived by private or public ferry boats that criss-crossed the bay from mainland Long Island to the various communities stretched along the long narrow strip of sand dunes that made up this island retreat for holidaying New Yorkers. The more affluent arrived and departed regularly by plane. However, no matter how they arrived on the island, residents and guests usually had to walk to and from their houses dragging wagons to carry their groceries, luggage, and all manner of goods deemed necessary to summer survival.

Only the sound of the rubber wheels bumping across the wooden slats of the long narrow boardwalk broke the uncanny silence. Dendre's feet were burning from the intense heat of the bare boards so she stopped and retrieved a pair of sandals she kept in the wagon and slipped them on. She had covered only a short distance and was approaching Gideon's vast studio when, much to her astonishment, she saw her husband emerge from it at a run towards the landing dock.

He seemed to glow with excitement. His light brown hair, streaked blond from the sun and mixed with strands of grey, shone in the brightness of the day, as did his tanned, muscular and seriously sexy body. He looked every inch the erotic soul, the passionate heart, a man familiar with both agony and ecstasy. The power of his passions, his grip on life, was awesome, more so because of his near-nakedness, save for the blue swimming trunks. But had he been dressed in a suit and tie it wouldn't have made much difference. It was all there in his eyes: large, of a brown so dark they were nearly black, and sparkling with life and intelligence. They were mischievous, sexy eyes set wide apart in a large square masculine face with a straight Roman nose, high cheekbones, a dimple in the right cheek.

For a brief moment Dendre was able to gaze into his eyes. He did not see her. It was as if she were invisible. That hurt. So much so that she stood still and watched him run, unable to utter a word. She blanked from her mind yet again that look she had seen too many times in Gideon's eyes: the thrill of the chase for someone other than herself. Dendre turned the little red wagon around and headed back to the house to finish her pineapple upside-down cake.

It was nearly two hours before Gideon and Adair walked arm in arm into Dendre's kitchen. Two of the girls, Pieta and Amber, had come in from the beach with a young man, a concert flautist who lived several houses away from the compound. Adam Soral on occasion played his flute for Gideon in the studio while he worked. Pieta and Amber, after a brief but friendly greeting to Adair, snatched their father away from her and dragged him over to Adam.

Dendre smiled across the room at Adair and told her, 'Nothing fancy but a good lunch. I'm glad you were able to come and share it with us.'

Adair smiled back, wondering at Dendre's composure. Surely she must understand after the six months of open affection Adair and Gideon had displayed for each other that they were seriously involved in both a loving and a sexual relationship? Adair could never quite decide if it was just composure or if Dendre was in fact much cleverer than she appeared to be. Was she hoping to ride out this affair as she had so many others? Well, not this one, Adair told herself.

It wasn't very often that she thought of Gideon's wife. But

somehow today she found herself taking stock of her riva
Dendre did have a good body, very sexy, and surprisingly
youthful-looking for a woman her age. For a few seconds
she imagined Dendre out of her black bathing suit, Gideon
poised lustfully over that body. Then she dismissed it from
her mind. Dendre simply did not exist for Adair as anything
other than the nearly invisible wife. She was, after all, no
threat, this drudge whose face was more interesting than
mannequin-beautiful, with the long aristocratic nose that
seemed to fill it. But the dark, nearly black, almond-shaped
eyes, full of passion and intelligence, appeared frozen in
a middle-class vacuum that stopped her from being more
than she was. How wasted the high cheekbones and lovely
sensuous lips, that long slender neck, because of Dendre's
lack of style. Adair saw in her a kind of inverted snobbery
and, no matter how well hidden, an arrogance. She believed
herself above cosmetics, designer labels, any sort – no matter
how restrained – of Fifth Avenue chic. She still dressed and
looked humdrum bargain-basement Brooklyn, this woman
whose husband's paintings fetched millions of dollars.

Adair felt pity for Dendre Palenberg. The younger woman
found everything about her pathetic: her enslavement to
Gideon, her obsessive love for her husband, her adoration of
domesticity which Adair saw as a trap that ate up a woman's
life. The way she behaved to Gideon in public irritated Adair
as well as much of the art world; to her he was just a husband,
not a genius. She was most definitely a bourgeois wife, not a
true muse. That was just fine with Adair who had no desire
to replace her. Adair had just the relationship she wanted
with Gideon. They met each other's needs, added to each
other's lives. Sex and intelligence, a passion for greatness
in art, bound them together. Not home-made mayonnaise.

Looking across the kitchen at Adair standing alone,

ng with youth and beauty and the bloom that comes
a woman has been made love to as well as fucked,
are realised for the first time that Adair was offering
deon everything that Dendre herself never could. For a
few seconds the two women gazed into each other's eyes
and Dendre felt Adair's indifference to her. She, Dendre,
Gideon's wife, was not even a rival to be dispensed with,
just an object to be ignored.

Dendre broke that gaze with the excuse that she had to go
to the larder for something. It took a great deal of self-control
not to lose her composure and run from the kitchen because
she sensed in that look Adair Corning's sheer disbelief that
Gideon could love this woman.

In the larder Dendre sat down on a butcher's block,
placed her hands over her face and took deep breaths to
regain her composure. Then she did what she always had
when another woman had come into their lives and Gideon
strayed: she blocked out her fear of losing him by coming
to the conclusion that a fling is not a wife, and *she* was
Gideon Palenberg's wife. The woman he could never live
without.

Dendre remained in the larder for a few more minutes,
thinking dispassionately about Adair Corning. It had been
that gaze that had thrown her off balance. It had somehow
undermined her denial of who this woman was and how far
she had infiltrated their lives.

She remembered seeing the impressively beautiful and
chic Adair Corning in the upper echelons of the artistic
circles the Palenbergs travelled in long before they ever met.
Dendre had watched her from a distance, this Bennington
graduate who had majored in art for most of her life, and
was the intimate friend of great painters and sculptors who
vied for her attention. She was the budding art historian with

something special to offer. Adair was fêted: a sharp wit who had in equal measure a fierce intelligence and a sureness of self, a sensuality that seduced, an independence that excited those men she wanted, got, and hung on to until she tossed them away when they no longer added anything to her life but only infringed upon it.

Dendre had for a long time envied her for the string of suitors craving her attention, even though it was well known that Adair had a penchant for older married men of great talent and power who embraced her and her ability to be a muse to them. She was a formidable presence in the art world, giving more than a few art historians a run for their careers.

Dendre thought her arrogant, this well-born daughter of a Washington Senator. It was not gossip but fact that she was wealthy in her own right from old family money that allowed her to live as she pleased, do anything she chose to with her life. At this time, that seemed to be being Gideon Palenberg's lover and muse. As Dendre sat alone, facing the reality of Adair Corning, she came to realise that the young and sensuous art historian had everything Gideon admired, wanted, and had missed out on in his wife as well as in his brief sexual liaisons. Adair was the whole package, the entire ball of string, and Gideon was in love with this young woman whom he had brought into his home and their family life.

All right, now she had faced it! Dendre's sigh was deep and troubled as she drew a curtain in her mind to block out what she had just seen. Dendre had always been brilliant at ignoring the more unpleasant intrusions into her life.

When she returned to her kitchen she saw Gideon surrounded by two of the girls and Adair. Adam was playing his flute. Gideon loved his daughters. He saw so much of

11

himself in them that it was a joy to be with them. Yet he could be stern with them too when it was called for. Now he was caressing Pieta's cheek. Amber picked up his hand and kissed it before wrapping his arm around her waist and leaning against him. It was a moment of tenderness that seemed to fill the room. But then, anything Gideon did always filled the room.

The happy party of people didn't see Dendre return or if they did they didn't acknowledge it. She watched as Gideon unwound himself from his daughters and, taking Adair by the hand, drew her tight against him. He stroked her hair and gazed briefly into her eyes. Dendre saw a spark of excitement in her husband's – lust for Adair. She ignored it and once more told herself he would never leave her. She was the mainstay of his life.

Because the girls were used to seeing Adair on their father's arm and in their lives, they took it as quite normal that he should embrace her. They were hardly naive about their father and the other women, who, for rather long periods of time, had drifted in and out of their lives. Rather they, like him, were charmed by Adair. She was an example to them of the chic and polish their mother ignored and most girls would like to have. Pieta, the youngest, was openly adoring of Adair; Daisy, at twenty-two, was dazzled by her youth and intelligence; while Amber, the eldest at twenty-four, saw her as the sophisticated woman she herself aspired to be.

The Palenberg girls loved their mother; she was home to them, ran their lives in the same way as Dendre's mother had once run hers. But they were, too, their father's daughters and more like him than their mother in every way. They had inherited fame and fortune and were able to go out into the world with everything their mother and their father never had

12

when they were young. Interesting girls, they each in their individual way intended to make their mark on the world as their father had, as Adair was doing. It was understandable they should be happy for her to be in their lives.

'Lunch is ready,' announced Dendre, and the group dispersed towards the dining room.

As she dropped home-made pasta into boiling water, Dendre felt once again in control of her happiness. Gideon and the girls were waiting to be nourished by the lady of the house. She smiled, remembering her adage, 'A fling is not a wife'.

Gideon stood by her side to remove the scarf from Dendre's head and rearrange the strands of her hair. She turned to face her husband, leaned forward and kissed him. He picked up a tea towel from the kitchen counter, gently wiped the perspiration from her face and affectionately caressed her shoulder. He slipped his hand under the strap of her bathing suit and caressed her naked breast, then her bottom. He had always liked her body but had stopped doing portraits of her long ago when the passion had gone out of his love for her.

He stepped a few paces away from his wife. Gideon felt in himself that aura of joy, excitement and powerful virility that he wore like a king wears his royal robe. He wanted to feel those things more intensely and Adair, the sex life they had together, her intelligence, gave that to him – not his wife and her pasta. Dendre gave him something else, domesticity, the enemy of the creative process, and it was slowly choking him to death.

'Slaving over food all day in this heat . . . why?'

Dendre was smart enough not to tell him 'for you'.

'Where's Kitty and Yukio? I suppose you gave them the day off?'

'No,' answered Yukio.

Gideon turned to see him and Kitty, Dendre's house staff, enter the kitchen followed by his own assistants.

'We've been putting up a dining pavilion on the beach. The table's set, the wine is cold, and we've come to tell you lunch is served.' Everyone reached for a serving dish to carry back to the beach.

Gideon was delighted. He liked nothing better than dining with his extended family under a roof of woven reed mats set up by the water's edge. It would be one of those long, leisurely lunches after which they would lie on the sand or walk along the beach. The added bonus was that today Adair was here. He intended to disappear down the beach with her, for them to swim in the ocean together, have sex in the water and lie in one another's arms at the water's edge letting the waves wash over them. He was besotted with Adair. They were besotted with each other.

For several seconds he contemplated his wife. Her body language was subtle, shy. There was about it a youthful vigour, a certain overt coolness that suggested the fire that burnt within. It was still attractive to him for the way she used it. Not a beautiful face but an interesting one. Fascinating to paint for the hidden depths of her character, but it had always been her selfless devotion and love for him and the girls, her complete submission to Gideon, his fame and fortune, that had kept their marriage strong. He was her life. Once he had loved that. Now he hated it.

Gideon carried the massive bowl of pasta down to the pavilion. The heat and humidity were still oppressive but they were dining three feet from the water's edge and the light breeze, the sound of the waves rolling near their feet, gave some relief. Dendre took her seat at the foot of the table, Gideon the head, and luncheon commenced.

14

Dendre looked down the length of the table presided over by her husband. He looked so young, so vital, the air electric with his personality. He could be so very amusing, and was during lunch, managing to raise laughter all around. Art world stories kept tumbling out. Adam played his flute. And Adair! She shimmered with beauty and sensuality and wore her swimsuit and her charm like a matador his cape. Some people from The Pines, the community of houses further down the beach, were walking along the water's edge and asked politely, and with some awe at seeing the great man, if they might take a photograph of the lunch party. To Dendre's surprise Gideon gave his consent and asked if they would send him a print. They bubbled over with delight.

Replete with food, wine and good cheer, most of the party fell asleep on the sand under beach umbrellas. Adair and Gideon set off on their walk down the beach. It was dusk before they returned to the pavilion where Dendre was serving tea and cakes. Their long absence from the party caused not the least embarrassment to Gideon's wife or the others having tea. They were used to his appearances and disappearances.

The sound of the sea plane circling the house on the sand dunes above the pavilion curtailed tea for Adair. There were hurried goodbyes, kisses from some of the guests, and a thank-you to Dendre for another splendid feast. All three Palenberg girls accompanied Adair and Gideon across the narrow strip of island to the bay where the plane was waiting to take her back to New York.

On the plane Adair slipped into a dreamy state, a half sleep, where she could conjure up visions of the sexual encounters she and Gideon had shared that day in his studio and on the beach. The drone of the plane's engine lulled her into desire for more. She tingled with excitement, felt a

wave of sexual desire course through her. Adair wanted to
come again, right there and then, in a copious and powerful
orgasm.

Gideon could bring her to moments of such exquisite joy
that coming down from the heights was not easy. So she
relived every moment of their day's sexual encounters,
coming and coming again in the darkness of the cockpit.
She bit into the back of her hand to stifle a scream of
pleasure, her body tensed, she held her breath and came
once more, and it was over. At last she was down from
that rarefied place, sexual nirvana. Having a magnificent
orgasm without Gideon was a kind of reassurance that she
was not dependent on him to reach such erotic peaks.

He was the most powerful man she had ever known. He
ate his women up and spat them out without even knowing
what he was doing, and Adair had no intention of being
used like that. He had only one true love, one real passion:
his work. Adair and Gideon had talked about this and he'd
admitted it was true. All the women in the world could be
sacrificed at the altar of his creativity.

She laughed in the darkness of the plane. She was as
strong a woman as he was a man. Together they fed each
other's lust and intelligence, revelled in their independence
and understood each other's work as no other person before
them had. For them the thrill of the male-female chase would
always be on. It was inspiring and a little dangerous because
they were playing with high stakes: the erotic, love and
super-egos.

Chapter 2

Dendre was, of course, sitting at table number one on the ground floor of the Guggenheim Museum. The museum had never looked more splendid, more vital, than it did tonight, hung with no artist's work but her husband's. The Guggenheim was honouring Gideon Palenberg with a retrospective of his life's work: painting, sculpture, collage, assemblage. It had taken three years for the museum to organise the exhibition and weeks to install the lighting: pinpointing every work of art to the edges of its canvas, spotlighting the sculptured pieces. Soft, dim lights a few inches off the floor to walk by, otherwise darkness, only added to the experience of being enveloped by Gideon Palenberg's genius. The ground floor, where invited guests were dining and chatting, was illuminated by thousands of flickering candles. It was an occasion few who were privileged to be there would ever forget.

Dendre knew what she was going to hear. As a matter of protocol, she had been told what to expect. The State Department and the highest echelons of the art world liked their events to run smoothly. And yet, when her husband's name was called out as the recipient of the Medal of Honour for his contribution to American Art by the President of the United States, she was somehow amazed that he should rise and make his way to the circular dais. The entire room rose

17

to its feet to give Gideon a long standing ovation. There were bravos, a stamping of feet. And a voice in her head shouted: 'Gideon, this honour is just as much mine as yours, you bastard!' That was very unlike the painter's wife, completely out of character. It quite shocked her.

What had precipitated such an unthinkable thought? He had received honours for his work from most countries; many less splendid retrospectives and exhibitions than this one could boast that the artist had been there with the museum staff, working on the hanging of the exhibition. But it had been Gideon's policy, until this evening, to stay away from the receptions, sending his regrets and his dealer, Haver Savage, to accept any honour on his behalf. It was not so much that he disdained the social side of the art world, more that Gideon knew his own worth, the measure of his contribution to contemporary art, and felt he could better use his time and energies than in charming the people who were praising him.

Dendre had always admired and agreed with the reticence that set him apart from the merry-go-round of art honours and grand exhibitions. Now, on this very public occasion, face to face with the immense power her husband wielded, the praise showered upon him, she felt diminished yet further by his ego, his massive success.

Was this the man who for years only visited galleries and museums early in the morning when hardly anyone was out viewing so as to avoid the public? Hardly! This Gideon, her Gideon, whom she had shielded from every intrusion into his life so he might live and work in peace and quiet, seemed to be lapping up every moment of the triumphant evening. She felt for the first time in all their years together that her husband was pulling away from her.

Dendre wished he had accepted the honour without all the

fuss of black tie, evening dress, and embarrassing praise from a country that had shunned his work for so many years when they were young. Gideon had been as fine a painter then as he was now. His canvasses of that period were more sought after than any of his subsequent works and almost never came on the market. When they did, they commanded prices of tens of millions of dollars. But where were the museums and patrons and admirers when she and Gideon had really needed them? When she had worked two jobs to keep him in paint while they survived on food parcels from her mother, who brought them over from Brooklyn to Gideon's cold-water studio in an abandoned building? Oh, yes that medal was *theirs*, not Gideon's, and once on that dais she convinced herself her husband would tell the world so.

Dendre looked around the table at the other luminaries of the art world, paying homage to her husband and oh-so-politely ignoring her. She suddenly resented the looks of adoration her three daughters directed towards their father as she did the others at the table, chattering animatedly with Adair while limply shaking her hand and looking over her shoulder, trying to make eye contact with someone more important. She felt not embarrassment but disdain for Adair, the great man's mistress, the not-so-well-kept secret, greedy for the limelight.

If not on Gideon all eyes had been on Adair because when he had risen from his chair, he had first clasped Dendre's hand for one brief moment then given an intimate hug and kiss to the young, sensuous and seductive Adair Corning.

Momentarily Dendre lost sight of Gideon in the crowd, and then quite suddenly he was there, on the dais. A wave of silence ran through the room that was broken by the sound of chairs shuffling as people sat down.

The President made his announcement. 'I have followed

your work since I was a young man at college, sir, and it is an honour for me to bestow on you, Gideon Palenberg, your country's highest honour for achievement in the world of arts and letters.' And he presented Gideon with the Medal of Honour, dangling from its red, white and blue silk grosgrain ribbon.

Gideon received it in his hands rather than round his neck. Here, thought Dendre, is the moment of truth. It's now that he will acknowledge that it is *our* moment of triumph. And her heart felt glad again for this extraordinary man whom she loved beyond measure. The man she had nurtured so the world might be enriched by his life and work.

The guests rose once more from their chairs and stood silently, ready to hear a speech of gratitude from one of the twentieth century's most important painters. Dendre rose from her chair along with them. Her knees felt weak with anticipation: the reward she so rightly deserved for her lifetime's obsession, loving her husband, was practically within her grasp. She watched Gideon take stock of the faces round the room. His eyes lingered longer on some than others. He was as he always was: a dazzling figure. One could feel the power and passion of the man. The vitality and intelligence behind those sparkling eyes. Finally he smiled at his admirers, turned on his heel and acknowledged the President with a slight inclination of his chin. Then, head high, he walked from the dais having uttered not a word.

It took several seconds for the guests to realise that was it. He had nothing to say to them collectively. Was this an insult? Pure arrogance? Or was he just being true to himself, saying with his silence what he had always claimed: that he had nothing to say, it was all there in his paintings? He had no one to thank, would not share this moment with anyone. It was his and his alone.

Dendre watched him walk through the crowds of people, stopping to accept a handshake here, a kind word there. She watched him kiss a famous collector of whom he was extremely fond. Men patted him on the back. Glittering women, gowned and jewelled on a grand scale, looked at him adoringly. The President of the United States, standing alone on the dais, looked somewhat confused as to what to do. He had expected a graceful acceptance speech and to be able to banter and charm the great painter, win over the Republican moneyed glitterati that a Democratic President would like to turn. But instead he seemed to have paled into insignificance next to the fêted artist.

Dendre saw her daughters and Adair pushing their way through the milling guests to reach Gideon but she didn't move, had not made even the least gesture of excitement when her daughters had kissed her on the cheek and tried to drag her along with them. Momentarily, she was traumatised by loneliness, the sight of her life racing away from her: Gideon, surrounded by praise and laughing heartily with strangers, her children weaving their way round the tables to reach their father. Adair, very nearly next to Gideon, turned round to look over her shoulder towards Dendre.

For a fleeting moment she saw herself in the younger woman – in love, full of joy for her man – and was overwhelmed with desire to be possessed by the object of her obsession as the lovely Adair was now.

Several people approached her briefly with congratulations and Dendre went through the motions of politeness but she felt as if she were somewhere else, as if she were there in body while her heart and soul hovered somewhere else in the room. Her brother Orlando approached her and kissed her on the cheek, placing an arm round her shoulders. She hardly saw him through her anxiety, this elder brother

21

to whom she had been close all of her life and was still, in spite of their having gone their separate ways during her formative years.

'Did you ever dream, when you first brought Gideon home to Brooklyn in those early days, that a night like this would be yours? That he would become a living legend?'

Dendre had no idea what to say to Orlando. Was he blind? Did he not see that she had been left behind for a younger, more beautiful woman who was everything she had never been? She wanted to burst into tears, she was so overwhelmed by self-pity. But Dendre was strong, hardened by compromise, and composed enough to hold back her tears. She did not need to answer Orlando because Adair arrived to stand between them.

Her first words were to Dendre. 'Come join us. We didn't mean for you to be left here alone at an empty table. We're table hopping. Join in the fun.'

Dendre could feel Adair's pity and found it embarrassing. She needed no sympathy from her husband's mistress. But before she could say anything Adair had switched her attention to Orlando. They hugged each other, she kissed him. He was full of enthusiasm for Gideon and his family, the evening, the honour that had been bestowed on the artist.

Orlando looked over Adair's shoulder at his sister. How had Dendre hoped to keep a man like Gideon with her casseroles and home-baked bread, slavishly keeping his houses in order while women like Adair were inspiring his virility, his heart, his soul even? He felt no pity for his sister, merely empathised with her situation and wondered how true love for her husband had turned into an obsession that was mostly to do with herself and largely disregarded the extraordinary man to whom she was married.

He knew it, as did Gideon. The two men had been close

ever since Gideon had married Dendre and over the years had discussed, if only in passing, such things. That his sister and brother-in-law loved each other there was no doubt. That things were different between them now was obvious. That she was his rock, the hub of his life, had been true, what Gideon had wanted and needed and probably still did. How, then, had they drifted so far apart? Dendre's passion for Gideon had slowly ebbed away in the day-to-day reality of living together. Somehow she had transferred those feelings into making a better soufflé, keeping his public at bay, his children as reflections of herself. Dendre had turned into her mother. What Gideon wanted now at this time of his life was to be renewed every minute of every day, not by a perfect meal but by a bright, self-possessed young beauty with whom he shared an adventurous sex life.

Orlando had dined with Adair and Gideon several times unknown to Dendre. In each case when their paths crossed it had been accidental: once in California at the museum where Gideon was hanging a one-man show; once in London when they came across each other in the dining room of the Connaught; again in Paris when he'd bumped into Adair on the Avenue Montaigne and she'd insisted he join them for a lunch of oysters and a bottle of Chablis. He could understand Gideon's passion for Adair; she was a risk to be taken, an adventure in everything she was – the way she moved, her intelligence, her sensuality. She made Gideon feel young. Tweaked his creative soul. Hers was a sexuality to rise to. She was everything a man like Gideon needed to feed his voracious appetite for work and sex, the sheer joy of living.

Orlando had seen Gideon devour his sister, her obsession for her husband kill off the very things Gideon had loved and adored her for, and yet still they had something together.

A history? Love? Who knew? Until tonight he'd thought Dendre would be able to hold her marriage together.

Now, with Adair still in his arms, looking over her shoulder at his sister, he sensed that could no longer be. There was something, a look in Dendre's eyes, that made him understand that tonight, his country's tribute to Gideon, and the manner in which the art world luminaries were paying homage to her husband and oh-so-politely ignoring her, had isolated her from her obsession. Reality was coming in on her at a hundred miles an hour. But he knew his sister, he understood obsession, it wasn't quite over for Dendre yet.

Adair released herself from Orlando's hug and approached Dendre. 'Come on, we've joined up with Rauchenbourg and Jim Dine, and Gideon is holding court. Even the President and First Lady have joined the table. It's not fair you should be left out.'

Dendre regained her composure. She was still the wife of Gideon Palenberg, the man being fêted this evening, and Adair was right, she belonged with her husband. 'Did Gideon send for me?' she asked.

'Of course,' was the young woman's reply.

A blatant lie! And all three acknowledged it. A look passed between the two women and both knew that Adair could afford to be generous. She was after all the victor, behaving not like a clandestine lover but as a wife might towards a former mistress. She had won Gideon's affections, his passion, his love, from Dendre and there could be no cover-up or let's-pretend about that between them.

But Dendre was not without a certain power of her own in the art world. Famous painters' wives held a special position as muse-cum-housekeeper. Admirers of a painter's work could hope that through them there might be a direct link to the artist when other avenues were closed. Dendre had always been aware of that and had capitalised upon it sparingly, but used it nevertheless. Her aloofness from the art world at first awoke interest in her but unfortunately that interest soon waned for Dendre Palenberg had very little to offer as an individual. Most people saw her now as her husband's shadow. There were, however, exceptions and one of them approached Dendre now.

Ben Borgnine was a respected art dealer with famous galleries in New York and London. Adair greeted him with her usual charm and introduced him to Orlando. He greeted her brother but went straight to Dendre and kissed her on the cheek. Taking her hand in his he told her, 'Tonight could never have happened without your years of support for Gideon. Many congratulations.'

His words were a soothing balm to her jagged emotions. They gave her strength. Ben always gave her strength, made her feel whole, something special. They had known each other for years. He was obsessed with Gideon's work and had showed him many times in group exhibitions at his galleries. His greatest ambition was to be Gideon's sole agent, something Gideon would never allow. He already had the best dealer in the world who suited him perfectly.

Ben Borgnine was a young fifty-year-old who looked more the Steve McQueen man of action than the smooth, erudite, fiercely clever art dealer he in fact was. He had been Dendre's first lover. She had been seduced by Ben many years before and the two had kept up an on/off affair that had given Dendre an escape from the reality of her life and her overwhelming love for her husband. It had saved her marriage by allowing her a secret life of sexual fantasy and adoration. Her fragile ego had needed that and it had been no threat to her marriage. It had nothing to do with Gideon and her love for him.

Ben Borgnine had a knack for appearing when she most needed him. Dendre's heart lifted as she told Orlando and Adair, 'You two go ahead, we'll follow.' With that she poured two glasses of champagne and handed one to Ben.

'Some night, Dendre,' he told her as he touched the rim of his glass to hers. 'Not only *are* you a marvel, but you *look* marvellous.'

'Do I?'

He laughed. 'Every inch the grand dame, painter's wife.'

She laughed. 'I did try! If you only knew what this dress cost. More than my whole wardrobe.'

'Dendre! Your husband sold a painting to the Tate last week for four million dollars, and you're still penny pinching? Darling, you left Brooklyn a long time ago, hasn't anyone told you that?'

'My daughters, every day. But then they can afford to laugh at my penny pinching – they have a wealthy mother and father.'

It was just that sort of light banter that had made her take notice of Ben Borgnine, all those years ago. She had watched him with beautiful young women whom he wore on his arm like trophies and been flattered when he paid her attention, when he seduced her to his bed. There was sexual heat between them right from their first clandestine liaison and after fifteen years it had not wavered.

Whenever Ben saw her naked, the many studies Gideon had painted of his wife over the years flashed before his eyes. He had wanted the woman in those portraits long before he ever met and bedded Dendre. And he wanted her now just as much. Not only her body but her appearance of passivity added something more to his lust for Dendre. In sex one reached into the heart and very soul of Dendre Palenberg. He always marvelled how few people could see that. They never

26

seemed to get past the interesting but not beautiful face. Ben was one of the few who could understand Gideon's attraction to her, why his paintings of her were as erotic and powerful as they were. Why people stood crowded in front of pictures in museums all of which bore the same title: 'Woman', by Gideon Palenberg.

Love never came into it because of her obsession with Gideon. But sex did. Ben and the circumstances of their affair had served Dendre well. He was only the second man she had ever slept with, Gideon having been the first, and he, like her husband, could turn off the outside world for her, make her feel like the Empress Erotica whom any man would want. With Ben, as with Gideon, she could give herself up sexually and ride her orgasms into an ecstasy that was more powerful and sublime than anything else she had experienced. In sex she was able to run wild, live fully, in a way she denied herself otherwise, caught up in her love for Gideon.

Dendre's adultery had been hard for her to accept at first. That was why their affair had been on/off yet remained a constant in her life. She listened to the hum of the crowd, the string quartet playing Vivaldi, then she focused her attention on the table where Gideon was holding court. She watched him lean across to whisper something in Adair's ear. Adair smiled seductively, nodded and moved away from the table, followed closely by Gideon. Dendre reached for Ben's hand and held it tightly as she watched them leave.

It was only a short distance from the Guggenheim down Fifth Avenue to Adair's spacious flat overlooking Central Park. The lift opened directly into her own private hall. From there Adair slid open a pair of oversized sixteenth-century wooden Japanese doors whose painted tigers looked ready to pounce, so skilled was their execution. The vast drawing room was in darkness with a view of the New York skyline, the moon and stars, as backdrop. Together, arm in arm, Gideon and Adair turned away from it and walked to the bedroom.

Gideon never found Adair as attractive with clothes on as he did naked. It was not only because of her spectacularly sensuous and near-perfect body: high, full and rounded breasts, provocative nipples made even more so by the large plum-coloured nimbus surrounding them, the slender waist and hint of roundness at her hips, the curve of her back and high bottom. She had kind of slender lusciousness. Her patch of pubic hair intrigued, excited him to want to explore that inner, most private part of Adair: her lust.

Adair's long slender arms, those perfect thighs and legs that seemed to go on forever, long slender feet . . .

Both naked now, Gideon took Adair in his arms and carried her to the bed where he lay her down on her side. She made no move towards him, not a kiss. She never fondled him. It was she who wanted to be caressed, made love to. It was she who wanted to be wakened, to be made to come alive. Gideon kissed her breasts, licked her nipples, nibbled and sucked on them, slipped his fingers along the slit between her legs to fondle her soft and seductive hidden lips. She whimpered.

He turned her on her stomach and raised her on to her knees; he placed a pillow under her head. For a few seconds he watched her make herself ready for him: she leaned upon her forearms and moved her legs further apart the better for him to get between them. Then he mounted her and took her slowly from behind. Sank himself deep inside her, and with his hands round her waist fucked her with long, easy strokes. She clung to him with her cunt, hungry for more. Her body tensed, her heart raced, and she came in a strong and copious orgasm. She called out in her moment of ecstasy for more and more and Gideon took her again and again until he went quite mad with lust for her. He wanted to fuck her into oblivion which he did. When he came he had taken possession of her totally. *They* had taken possession of each other. Yes, in her own seductive way, in sex, she could do that to Gideon. It always surprised them, this sexual power she had over them.

Lust and sex, all things erotic, were the norm for Adair. She had been taught that by Gideon and so craved sex such as she was having now: where her every orifice was ready to receive male lust in its most rampant and exciting form. To hold the seed, the taste of a man, to be filled by him, was for her the most sublime of all the passions that can happen between a man and a woman.

When they returned to the museum no more than half an hour had passed. People were roaming up and down the ramp that wound round the exhibition. The tables had been cleared away but there was no sign of the evening breaking up.

Dendre, who had been searching the galleries for Gideon, caught sight of Orlando and her three daughters and felt very proud of them. They were the beauties she had never been; they had the poise and charm of their father, even a touch of his arrogance. They would fare well in this world they adored, giving it a run for its money as she had never done.

At last she saw that Gideon had returned. He was standing with several other people, his arm round Adair, caressing her bare shoulder.

Chapter 3

'He has achieved more in his lifetime than most men and he is still comparatively young. He's belonged to the world for a very long time and it's admirable how you've managed to handle that,' said Orlando as he slipped an arm round his sister's shoulders and kissed the top of her head.

Ben and Dendre had found him standing in front of a portrait of Dendre that was on loan from the Museum of Contemporary Art in Paris for the Guggenheim's retrospective. His arms had been folded across his chest and he had been contemplating the image before him when he felt his sister's presence next to him.

Dendre looked at her portrait. How Gideon had loved her then! She leaned against her brother and told him, 'I was Dendre Moscowitz, a nineteen-year-old innocent, when I sat for that portrait. Only tonight do I realise that after all those years since I first set eyes on Gideon, and with everything we have been through together, I have in many ways never stopped being that innocent – that is, until tonight.'

There was something in the tone of her voice that neither Ben nor Orlando had ever heard before. Was it sorrow, regret, even self-pity? Ben could have understood any of those emotions, knowing what life had been like married to Gideon. But no. This passionate woman had none of those things in her tone of voice. It was instead flat, icy indifference he heard. For the first time in all the years he had known her he realised she had seen it all, the reality of her relationship with Gideon. Every day, every hour of her life with him. Dendre had deliberately blinded herself to the battle she had been fighting all her married life – her obsessive love for her husband and his tyranny. Now a crisis was looming and Ben sensed there was nothing he could do to help her. It was time to retreat.

He raised her hand and kissed it. 'Not all that innocent, I think. Maybe an innocence of convenience. We've most of us at one time or another used that to get us by. There are the Bettles – I must have a word with them. Will you excuse me? Come and have lunch with me as soon as you can,' he told her, and then he was gone.

Orlando too picked up on the strangeness of her behaviour: not being with Gideon at a time like this, that tone in her voice, her sudden avowal of how very naive she had been. Orlando, a very clever doctor, had hinted through the years about obsessive love, how she had found a way to control Gideon through it. But she had never taken those hints on board, had always been too lost in her obsession, too rapt in the fantasy she had created for herself as Mrs Dendre Palenberg, wife of one of the world's greatest living artists.

'Dendre, is something happening that I should know about?' asked Orlando.

'I think you do know about it. I imagine the whole world knows about it. It's always the wife who's the last to hear,' was her reply.

'Let's go over there away from this crowd,' he suggested.

As Orlando walked with his sister to a bench just inside the entrance to the museum he was aware of other men's eyes upon her and saw her as a sensuous creature, sexy yet incredibly controlled. She had never seemed that way to him before. It quite shocked him. He was used to seeing his sister as a loving woman, a solid nourisher of her husband and family who obsessed over her man in spite of his many adulterous relationships, his at times despotic behaviour. Orlando had always thought her a proud woman who could endure everything Gideon could put her through because she believed her husband loved her more than any of his conquests. How many times had she told him that? He could not help but wonder if tonight she still believed it.

Once sitting on the bench, Dendre turned to her brother and said, 'You always knew, didn't you?'

'Knew what, Dendre?'

'That he didn't love me in the same way I love him. He didn't feel about our marriage as I have always done.'

'All your married life I've tried to tell you that, my dear,' said Orlando, taking her hand in his to comfort her. 'But why are we talking about this now, on this glittering occasion? Not exactly the right time and place, I think.'

'Because this evening, for the first time, as Gideon walked away from me to receive his Medal of Honour, I realised that he *never* loved me more than the others. That our marriage is no more than a convenient arrangement for him.'

'I would have put it differently, and will at another time.'

'No, Orlando, now. I need to know, to try and understand what Gideon and I were all about before he leaves me for Adair.'

'Dendre! Do you know he will?'

'In the marrow of my bones. So, how would you describe it? This marriage that became my life and is ebbing away?'

Orlando saw no point in being evasive. At last she was prepared to listen and hear, to look and see, through the window that had opened into her obsession.

'Dendre, it's arrogant of you to think that a husband must

love a wife in the same way as she loves her husband. Arrogant more than naive, my dear. The ego rather than the heart making demands. It's very rarely that husbands and wives love in the same way. You mustn't do anything rash about Gideon or your marriage. You claim you can see it now for what it has always been. I'm not so sure you do.'

Dendre was about to speak but he stopped her. 'Please let me finish. That Gideon loves you there is no doubt. That he is happy in his marriage, I have no doubt about that either. But . . . as much as he loves those two aspects of his life, he also hates them. Gideon has a love-hate relationship with you and marriage. He always has had. And if you would take the time to think about that, you would realise you've always known it.'

'Is that what people think?' she asked, a note of astonishment in her voice.

'A few, possibly, but I wouldn't have thought it was common knowledge. He's covered up his feelings pretty well. Or, more to the point, your actions always made sure it was something you never recognised, and you saw to it that no one else did either.'

'Am I that clever?'

'People lost in their obsession can become very clever, devious even, to sustain their fantasy world.'

'I never dreamed Gideon hated me and our marriage as much as he loved it. That is, not until our eyes met tonight when he rose from his chair to walk away from me. I saw it again when he turned away from me to the applause and that standing ovation. It was as if he was screaming at me, "In spite of you, love, marriage!" I waited for him to acknowledge me from that dais, one word of any sort for the world to hear. Nothing. Just nothing. In a way that was the cruellest blow he's ever delivered to me.

'He beamed for the recognition of his life's work. It was a look of love and passion such as he has never had for me. He has them for himself, his work, his daughters and Adair, but never for me. You are quite right, he hates me and marriage even though he also loves me. Why? What have I ever done to him to generate such feelings?'

'You trapped him in a bourgeois life – the death knell for a great artist who has to be free. You took him over with your love and possessiveness, became a tyrant with a wooden ladle, a martyr to nappies. You were a bodyguard who kept the world at bay. You held him prisoner, darling, and still from within the cage you kept him in, he learned to fly away from you anyway.'

'Are you telling me that throughout all those good and bad times down the years, I have been deluding myself? That he has never loved me as he now does Adair?'

'Yes, I'm sorry to say.'

'I can't accept that, Orlando.'

'I know. But eventually you will and then it will be all right again for both of you,' he told her.

Her laugher was bitter. Orlando caressed her hair and told her, 'This night is going to go down in art history. It was a mistake to ruin it for yourself.'

'I won't bear the brunt of that accusation. Gideon ruined it for me.' And, having said that, she rose from the bench, trembling.

Orlando was on his feet at once, comforting her. 'It will do you no good to have people see you in this state, Dendre. Especially Gideon. You do pick your times to wake up, tonight of all nights! I don't want you hurt any more than you already are, so please, for the sake of all concerned, no public scene.'

She gave a nervous laugh. Fighting back tears, she told her

brother in the saddest voice he had ever heard, 'It must be a family trait, being able to blind oneself from reality, because now you're doing it. Gideon is walking away from me and our marriage forever, and he's doing it blatantly in front of everyone here. He has it all, everything he has ever wanted, and on a grand scale. My worst fear from the first day we met and I fell in love with him is being realised in front of the whole of all America: he is leaving me behind. You see those TV cameras? That woman next to him with adoring eyes? That's not me, is it, Orlando? Our three daughters standing behind their father . . . I'm not there with them, am I?'

'Come then, let's join them,' he suggested.

'Why?'

'Because you've played out this scene one way or another many times and got on with your life with him.'

'Yes, that's true.'

'Then what makes tonight different from any of those other times?'

'I discovered tonight, when he failed to acknowledge to the world my part in his life and work, that I deserve better than the grudging love he doles out to me.'

'I can't dispute that,' said her brother.

'I think I could use a glass of champagne, Orlando.'

Dendre watched her brother walk away then melt into the crowd. She stood very much alone, still on the fringes of the throng, and searched the faces for Gideon and Adair. After several minutes she found him again. He was standing apart from a group of old friends, now famous artists like himself. They looked happy, glittering with pride, for each in their own way had made it big in the art world. True, none as big as Gideon had, but then none was as great an artist.

Gideon was lighting a large, fat Havana cigar. Never had he looked more magnificent than he did at that moment. He was still as he always had been, from that very first time she had seen him, every inch a charismatic figure. He was a volcano of a man, one who intrigued all who encountered him, commanded love and adoration from those who fell under his spell. She knew as she stood there looking at him across a crowded room that she would never be able to confront him, not in public nor in the privacy of their bedroom.

Aware now that there was no way she could challenge Gideon she brought herself under a semblance of control. She stopped trembling. Her fate had always been in his hands. Orlando was right; she need not make any moves about her love for Gideon or do anything about their marriage. She was no match for her husband. She never had been. He would do what he wanted to do and she would passively follow his every wish. She could do nothing but wait for her execution. That is, unless she saved her life and ran away.

Watching Gideon from a distance had a mesmerising effect on Dendre. She knew she could never run away. Then something quite inexplicable happened to her. Dendre, who by her very nature never looked at herself, did just that. Flashes of herself and her life became vivid pictures that ran before her like a strip of film she was forced to watch against her will.

Orlando returned with the glasses of wine. He saw something in Dendre so distant, so far removed from the present, that he spoke very nearly in a whisper so as not to jar her back too quickly from wherever she was.

'You seem so far away, in another world. Tell me that you're all right?' he begged.

She saw the deep concern in her brother's face, heard the anxiety for her in his voice, and reached out to caress his cheek. She took the glass of wine from his hand and slid her arm through his to walk him back to the bench where they had been sitting. The doors to the museum had been unlocked and streams of black-tied men and gowned women, the after-dinner guests, formed a slow but steady steam, flowing past brother and sister.

Dendre was hardly aware of them, she was far away. The vivid pictures of her life flashing before her had indeed transported her back to another time, another place, and the Dendre she had lost or misplaced somewhere along the line of loving Gideon.

'I *am* far away, back in Brooklyn when we were young, happy and secure. We neither knew nor wanted better than we had. Except for our youth, Mother's dreams and our arrogance, we might still be there.'

'Time doesn't stand still, Dendre.'

'No, but it lives on as memories or baggage that we carry with us all our lives. I keep getting flashbacks of how I was before I met Gideon. How comfortable our life was back in Brooklyn. It was our world then and how proud we were to have been born and bred there, be a part of Jewish Flatbush.

'I remember that first day I met Gideon on a park bench in Washington Square. It was a sunny day. I was eating the lunch Mamma had prepared for me: a sandwich of tongue and Swiss cheese on thick slices of rye bread with caraway seeds, a meat filled *K'nishe*, half a sour pickle, and for good measure three large *Kreplach*. I had bought a cup of coffee.'

Orlando began to laugh. 'One of Mamma's light lunches! She was a great cook but a lousy dietician.'

'But you never told her that?'

'No, never.'

'I never did either. She was our goddess, the comfort of our lives. Why would one offend Mother?

'Gideon was watching two men play chess when I first laid eyes on him. I thought him the handsomest man I had ever seen. He was like a Greek god, so big and proud. He emanated strength and sensitivity, both at the same time. He took a flask from the hip pocket of his jeans and I remember how shocked I was when he took several gulps from it and passed it on to the two players. I had never seen a man drink in the street before. It was a few minutes before he took notice of me. First my legs. He kept staring at my legs. I was wearing a lightweight black spring coat, it was early April. It had fallen open and so I closed it to cover my legs. He laughed aloud and walked directly up to me.

'"You were staring at me," he announced as a greeting.

'I was shocked at having been caught out. I told him, yes.

'He demanded to know why, so I told him that I had never seen a man drink in the street before. That's when he sat down next to me. He was very brazen. He opened my coat, draped it back and smiled. "You've got a great body, very sensuous," he said. "It likes the sun. Don't cover yourself up on my account. I'm very hungry. Will you share your lunch with me?"'

'And you did?' asked Orlando

'I didn't know what else to do. I moved away from him on the bench and tore open the paper bag. I used it as a place mat and spread the food out on it.

'"What a mountain of food for lunch! Do you always eat like this?" he asked.

'I thought that a strange question. Didn't everyone? I had always assumed they did. All our family ate like this, and our friends. To me it was the norm. I remember being surprised to learn that some people didn't.'

'"Don't you?" I asked him.

'"No, but I wish I did," he answered, and asked me what should he eat first.

'"I'd go for the sandwich," I told him, and handed him half. There was an inch of meat in it and half an inch of cheese, and – well, you know Mother. She never did know how to slice bread less than an inch thick.'

Orlando began to laugh. 'But Dad did.'

Then Dendre began to laugh too. 'Mamma always said that was because he spent a lifetime cutting up animal skins.'

'Funny, when we were children it never occurred to me what an odd couple they were and yet what a good marriage they had for all the differences in their characters.'

Dendre ignored the comment and continued with her story. 'Gideon asked me if I'd made the sandwich. I remember telling him, no, my mother was the cook in our household.

'"You eat extravagantly. I was brought up in a house of crustless sandwiches with only a hint of filling. I was always hungry," he told me.

'"And *I've* never eaten food like that," I told him.

'"And what is this?" asked Gideon while biting into a *Kreplach*.'

Dendre laughed aloud again. 'I explained it was a meat-stuffed ravioli and went on to describe the *K'nishe* too, as a baked meat- or potato-and-onion-filled pastry. Gideon had never even heard of Jewish food. He was ravenous. I watched him devour it all and still remember what delight I felt when he declared he liked Jewish food. So much so that I handed him my cup of coffee. When he was quite through eating and there wasn't a morsel of anything left, he smiled at me, and I fell hopelessly in love.

'"What's your name?" he asked me.

'"Dendre Moscowitz."

'"With a body like yours, Dendre, and a mother who cooks

like this, I might just marry you so I guess I'd better introduce myself. I'm Gideon Palenberg from St Louis, a starving artist who will one day rule the art world. Do you believe me?"

'"Yes," I told him. And I did, Orlando.

'"Come with me," he told me, and pulled me up from the bench by my hands. He gathered up the remnants of our lunch and, still holding my hand, we walked over to a bin and he deposited them there, rather ceremoniously I thought.

'I asked where we were going and he told me to his studio on Lower Broadway. He asked where I lived and laughed at my answer.

'"I should have guessed! You have a terrible Brooklyn accent. You should do something about it."

'I can see it all again, Orlando, as if it were yesterday. The way I pulled my hand away from his, the offence I felt at his criticism. The jealousy I experienced because he had an educated, cultivated accent.

'"I'm proud to have this accent," I insisted, "and to come from Brooklyn. It's the most wonderful of the city's five boroughs, except of course for Manhattan. But Manhattan is something else. Have you even been to Brooklyn?"

'I could see by Gideon's face that he was surprised, maybe a little amused by my passion for home. "No," he answered. "I only know that it's on the other side of the East River and you can see Brooklyn Heights from Manhattan."'

'You're babbling on about the past, dear. It's now you should be dealing with. The past is dead, and dead is dead,' Orlando told her not unkindly.

'Maybe for you, Orlando, but not for me. For me it's like re-running an old movie, one I must see. And who knows? Maybe a good look at where I was, where I came from, might validate the present. When you left Brooklyn for Harvard you really left your roots: me, Mamma and Papa, our perfect uncomplicated little world of families with big hearts, green parks, a world of culture and institutions of learning.'

'Yes, I did,' he readily admitted.

'And you're thinking I didn't, aren't you?' she asked.

'No, dear, you left but you took Brooklyn with you. Even now, right here, when you have the world as your playground, a husband honoured and respected beyond measure, you appear to want to diminish his life and work, yours too, in favour of a middle-class existence, the penny-pinching, safe life we led in our Brooklyn youth. It's a foolish person, Dendre, who after jumping the gully looks back. You might fall in.'

'Is that meant to be an insult?'

'No, dear, a warning. Now let's join Gideon and put this anxiety and unhappiness aside. It's so unlike you. I've never seen you like this, ever. It's out of character.'

Orlando simply did not understand. Something fundamental had happened to Dendre. The princess had awakened.

'You go ahead, there are several people I want to talk to. I'll catch up with you,' she told her brother.

As soon as he disappeared into the crowd, Dendre went to the cloakroom and produced the ticket that would claim her full-length chinchilla coat. Her father had not been a master furrier without her benefiting from his expertise and Gideon's generosity. She slipped into it and for once felt that the extravagant and luxurious work of art did indeed suit her. She left the museum and walked in the cold, crisp air for several blocks before she hailed a taxi to take her down town to West 27th Street close to the Hudson River. It was a dark, silent and dingy street save for the blinking bright neon light announcing 'The Sounion'.

Dendre walked from the street, deserted of people and traffic at that time of night, into the Greek restaurant to be met by the loud, screeching sounds of *bouzouki* music and the ebullient greetings of Dimitri Constantinos, the owner. She saw the redoubtable belly dancer, Yasmin, gyrating before a sea of mostly empty tables.

The Sounion came to life and was usually filled to capacity from midnight till five in the morning. Lonely Greek sailors, Greek ship owners, Greek Americans and homesick immigrants, even New Yorkers who had enjoyed their brief holiday taste of Greek life, used the place for a fix of hospitality, fun, and to gladden their hearts.

A snap of fingers, a rush of waiters, and Dendre was ushered to a front table where Dimitri removed her coat and pulled out a chair for her. Yasmin nodded a greeting and waved to Dendre without missing a beat or a shimmy.

'You are looking like a queen!' offered Dimitri, raising her hand to kiss her fingers.

'Always gallant,' she told him, a smile coming to her lips. It felt good to be here. This mad, funny place where she and Gideon liked to escape for a touch of the Greece they loved and missed when away from it too long. They liked the place for its not very good Greek food, fantastic Greek music, and the many Yasmins the place had worn out over the years. Dendre and Gideon loved The Sounion and liked Dimitri. Gideon enjoyed the camaraderie of the restaurant which was far removed from the art world. He liked the cross-section of humanity who ended their evenings here. He liked drinking hard with them and dancing by himself as some of the Greek men who gave their custom to the place were wont to do: a form of inner expression they had no qualms about displaying.

'Gideon, he is meeting you?' asked Dimitri.

'No. He's at a party. I needed to hear some Greek music, drink wine, watch Yasmin and raise my spirits. So here I am. Who knows? Gideon might arrive. It wouldn't surprise me. You know how he likes to dance when he's in a happy mood.'

This was not the first time that Dendre had arrived alone at Dimitri's place. He had many customers who liked, on occasion, to get away without their partners; the city's fast-lane livers who wanted only to hear the music and drift away into a world suspended beyond this time and place.

He returned only once to place in front of her a platter of fresh fruit peeled and sliced and arranged around a small bowl of thick amber-coloured honey and another of pistachio nuts, roasted open and salted.

Dendre watched a few minutes more of Yasmin's exotic dancing before the seductively plump and pretty young woman, heavily laden with dangling gold jewellery, rushed off the stage in a flutter of chiffon veils. And now the stars of The Sounion arrived: darkly handsome, dour-faced Greek *bouzouki* players. Instruments in hand, they took their seats and sat next to one another in a straight line facing the tables of admirers. A few minutes later the music was eating into Dendre's heart, and she fled back in time.

FIRE ISLAND,
NEW YORK CITY

1961–1993

Chapter 4

Dendre was trying to make some sense of what was occurring as Gideon Palenberg, holding her hand, pulled her through the Village and Lower Manattan to his studio. It was out of character for nineteen-year-old Dendre to allow herself to be picked up in the street by a man. She could make no sense of what was happening to her, her racing heart, the excitement of this adventure with a stranger.

She was overwhelmed by her feelings of sensual delight when he had boldly opened her coat and admired her figure then proceeded to eat her lunch with gusto. He had a look of lust in his eyes that triggered the memory of intimate sensations she had hitherto only experienced in the privacy of her bedroom, alone, while yearning to free herself from her virginity and get on with the business of sex and satisfaction.

Sex for Dendre was a fearful mystery. She wanted the security of marriage to legitimise the strong but well-suppressed libido which embarrassed her. Dating the Jewish boys from her neighbourhood, for the most part good-looking, clever, ambitious and sexy, she had looked on them first as husband material, only secondly as sex objects. Fear of being denounced as easy had determined her attitude to them. It reduced her sexual activity to nil, leaving her only to imagine sex which she knew nothing of and was eager to experience. The frustration of being a reluctant virgin but not having the least idea where to find the right man to whom to entrust her precious commodity (that was what her mother had taught her it was) had of late become an oppressive burden. Nineteen! It was time. She needed a strong, handsome and dashing man to rid her of her weighty problem. So between Washington Square and Lower Broadway Dendre fell in love.

'If you walked a little slower, I could keep pace with you,' she told Gideon.

Still with a tight grip on her hand, he stopped short and Dendre bumped into him. He laughed and told her, 'I am always rushing to something, someone, someplace. I want to live at the top of my life, experience everthing – and you're an adventure, something new to savour, like your mother's cooking!'

And with that he changed pace from a fast walk to a run, Dendre making an effort to keep up with him. After several blocks, they slowed down and Gideon placed an arm round her shoulders. They proceeded through the streets like that. Gideon, sensing her unease and lack of sophistication, found her enticing, so different from the beautiful all-American blonde-haired beauties he usually favoured on his arm and in his bed. He also perceived the latent sexual promise in Dendre Moscowitz. Where the face had more character than a fashion model's, the lush body lacked nothing. The way she moved was sensual, erotic even, so different from the still, almost introverted personality she displayed to the world. He was intrigued by the life of frustration he imagined she imposed upon herself.

As the streets they walked lost the charm of Greenwich Village, Dendre felt yet more unease about her adventure with this stranger. Filthy with rubbish and with few people visible, save for the drunken homeless lying on the pavement or leaning against mostly deserted buildings with boarded up doors and windows, there was here a frightening sense of poverty: of the heart and spirit and most certainly of the purse. There appeared to be no sign of life in the neighbourhood save for the several cats she saw scavenging, a few of whom streaked aggressively across the pavement in front of them while screeching for food. Where was the baker, grocer, cobbler, pharmacist? This was no neighbourhood community as Dendre understood one to be. This was a brick and stone desert.

At last Gideon stopped in front of a four-storey building. 'We're here. I can hardly wait to show you my work, hear what you think of it,' he told her as he pulled her tightly into his arms. He kissed her passionately before unlocking the heavy metal door that was scrawled with graffiti. The dismal street, the stench of poverty and neglect, all vanished from her mind with that kiss. Dendre felt giddy with passion, high on his vitality, full of excitement at the prospect of seeing his work. She was aware he had not released his grip on her as he pulled her into the lobby of the building she expected to be dark and dingy.

Gideon smiled at her expression of relief. It was all painted white, even the floor. There were several pieces of broken furniture painted in primary colours standing against the walls.

'All retrieved from skips,' he told her.

'Rubbish furniture that you've turned into sculpture,' she said.

Gideon saw the delight in her face. He had been right about her: she was hungry for life yet easy to train because there was something of substance to her. They would be good together.

'Assemblage,' he corrected. 'Useful Assemblage, pieces that hold all my worldly goods: clothing, food, the bits and pieces to keep my life going.'

The hall lights, naked bulbs hanging from long black flexes, cast a warm glow rather than bright light. There was such vibrancy, such energy, such a richness of life and spirit in each piece as it emerged from the shadows. They made Dendre instantly understand that their creator, her kidnapper, was a force of nature, a phenomenon that changed everything that came into contact with him. Dendre, seduced by what she was seeing, unwound Gideon's fingers from her wrist. She rubbed the soreness away as she walked around the room looking at his work.

'Don't waste your time here. This isn't my real work, merely the make-do household furniture of a poor starving artist.'

Gideon grabbed her once more, kissed her again, this time slipping his hands round her throat and caressing it before he slid them under the bodice of her dress to caress a breast. He felt her stiffen with fear but she did not run away. He smiled at this lack of sophistication. He liked her just that little bit more for it. He sensed she was overwhelmed by her feelings for him and liked that too. Taking both her hands in his, he raised them to his lips and kissed her fingers. Still holding on to her hand, he led her once more to where he was certain she wanted to be.

The rickety electric-blue wooden staircase they climbed was fiercely steep and cantilevered precariously off the wall. Dendre, whose fear of falling would ordinarily have kept her from mounting even the first stair, forgot to be afraid. She was too happy in her infatuation with Gideon to do anything other than bound up the stairs with him.

The huge open-plan loft was flooded with midday sunlight

from the vast windows at both ends of the room. It was nevertheless an eerie place with its high ceiling and cast-iron columns supporting the floor above. It smelled of damp, oil paint, linseed oil, turpentine. It was not so much an unpleasant odour as one that created a statement. This studio was an island of creative energy in the middle of Manhattan, a retreat, a place of isolation. The metal racks stacked with paintings, the white walls and orderliness of the space, gave Dendre a sense of organisation and strong purpose. It had an air of passion, dedication, endeavour on a massive scale.

Dendre caught a mere glance of some of the paintings set on the floor or leaning against the walls, a huge easel, a vast table where dozens upon dozens of squeezed-out tubes of oil paint lay neatly in rows, tins and glass jars holding worndown brushes of various sizes and lengths, a slab of glass obviously being used as a palette, as Gideon led her through the loft to an area where three mattresses lay piled one upon the other on the floor. They were made up with white sheets, a worn and tattered oriental rug thrown over as a coverlet. A table, or rather a wooden door set on two metal beer barrels, two wobbly wooden chairs in one corner away from the bed, a battered and noisy refrigerator and sad-looking cooker in another corner completed Gideon's living amenities save for the loo, a bookcase next to it and a double sink of chipped white enamel. There was not even a screen to hide them from view.

He turned her to face him and, still holding her hands, took a step back to look at Dendre. There was chemistry between them, an attraction that could not be denied, a silent but desperate need that had to be fulfilled. He let go of her hands to reach up and stroke her mass of long, black curly hair. He ran his finger down the bridge of her nose, traced her lips with it. Neither of them said a word.

He removed her coat and let it slip from his hands to the floor. He opened the buttons of her dress and slid it from her shoulders, letting it rest upon her hips. Then he observed her: breasts perfect in shape and size, nipples surrounded by a dark, deliciously decadent-looking halo that looked lustful, especially so for the pale firm flesh around it, skin soft as satin. He was enthralled by the ripeness, the readiness, of Dendre Moscowitz. He would paint her many times. She would represent for him the changing aspects of a woman in lust.

That chemistry between them became more intense. Dendre wanted to do something about it but had no idea what, or even how, to begin. She knew only one thing: she wanted to be possessed by Gideon. For him to love her as she had never been loved before, with passion gone wild. She could only think of giving herself over to him for his pleasure, for him to do anything, everything, that might give him such powerful gladness he would never want another woman. She was certain Gideon wanted her at that moment as he had never wanted another. It showed in the way he devoured her with his eyes and the glorious lust that shone in his handsome face.

And she was right. Gideon adored women, the female body, and sex on a grand scale. Sex and lust, the excitement of debauchery, took him to a place where he felt at home. Every aspect of orgasm was for him an elixir, a regenerating ambrosia fit for the gods. There was something so much more to this odd, immature yet sensual girl than her outward appearance indicated. He was falling in love with the mediocrity of Dendre Moscowitz's life, with the passionate secret soul that beat for him and him alone.

Gideon undressed in front of her, not hastily but because she could not take her eyes off him and he wanted her to savour every inch of his flesh. He was already erect, pulsating with desire to be taken over by her lips, to exchange sensual joy with her. The shock of seeing his ample penis so ready to take possession of her showed in her eyes. That look told Gideon she had never been so brazen with a man, so bewitched by a penis, so enamoured with the idea of sex in the streaming sunshine. He wanted her to fondle him, to excite his lust further. Nothing. She made no move towards him. Instead tears filled her eyes and her breathing became laboured. He knew instantly that passion and frustration were crippling her.

Gideon approached her and caressed her breasts, pinching her long thick nipples none too gently. Dendre moaned with pleasure and he kissed her intimately on the lips as he worked her dress down over her hips and tore the panties she was wearing first at one side then the other, slipping the cloth from between her legs. Naked now save for her white lace garter belt and stockings and still standing in her high-heeled shoes, Gideon viewed her as she had never been looked at before. Holding her by the hand, arm extended straight out, he walked around her.

'I'm going to paint you. Many times. Make you the most famous model the world will ever have known. You're magnificent in your lust. You have a very sexy body. I want the world to look at you and see how glorious a fuck you are, how a sexual woman can nurture lust and love, in herself and her man.'

Dendre was on fire. Over and over again she kept begging silently, Oh, please God, let him take me now. Please, now. The waiting to feel him inside me is too painful to bear. Now, please.

Gideon pulled her down on to her knees. 'You're a delicious creature and I'm going to take you places you've never been, make you come until all your pent-up sexual energy is satisfied – and then from there take you further than you have ever been. I'm going to make you mine forever, and leave no room in your heart and soul for anyone else but me. Do you believe me?'

'Yes,' she told him, and prayed he meant what he said.

'Then show me why I should do that?' he challenged.

Dendre caressed his thighs, ran her fingers over his thick patch of dark blond pubic hair then the inside of his thighs, but she never touched his penis. It surprised Gideon that she was cock-teasing him. He was past young women who played that game. If it had been anyone else he would have given up on her right then and there and seen her out of his studio, never to return. But Dendre . . . a teaser who never delivered? It didn't fit with her sincerity, the purity of spirit he sensed she had, her generosity, the passion and lust he saw in her eyes.

'Why do you look away from my sex when you want it? Dance around my penis with fondling hands and fingers like some cheap tease? You and I, we're not playing that game and we both know it,' he told her as he placed the fingers of her hand round his member and ran her hand back and forth over it. With the palm of the other placed under his large and handsome testicles, he wrapped her fingers round them so that she cupped them and could caress them.

His sighs were of the ultimate in pleasure and he told her, 'Oh, yes. How marvellous you make me feel. You're a delight in giving and loving.' And he closed his eyes, savouring her every caress.

Dendre felt a rush of power and strength coursing through her veins, her flesh. She came instantly and reached a moment of pure sexual nirvana. Once that moment passed she understood she had found the man she wanted to give herself to, now, at this moment, and for always.

Gideon was surprised by his own words and feelings. It was true, this was no game, no street pick-up as he had thought it would be when he first saw her. They wanted each other, to be in each other's lives. He was amazed that she should have captured his heart when other, more beautiful and exciting women had not. He felt good in her hands. Sensations of sexual bliss took him over, body and mind. He liked the way she caressed him, fondled his testes. He imagined her holding them in her soft, warm, satiny mouth, licking them like a pussy cat.

Now for Gideon the excitement of sex had to move on. Still standing, he caressed the top of her head and told her, 'I wonder if women know just how good that feels to a man? You're lovely, I like the way you love me.' He bent down and kissed her on the lips, licked them until they parted, then standing tall again he placed his hands over hers and directed the tip of his penis across her lips, back and forth, several times. Her lips parted. She licked him, at first hesitantly but then erotic passion, a hunger to taste more of him, took over and she sucked him gently into her mouth.

Overcome by her actions, fear of the unknown, her out-of-control behaviour, she hesitated and looked pleadingly into his eyes. That was the moment he took command of their lust and her life and Dendre relaxed into passivity. Each of them understood that rules had been set, roles delineated. She would love him as no other woman in this world could or would and he would love her for that.

'You've never done this before, had oral sex?' he asked not unkindly as he withdrew.

'No,' she answered, hardly above a whisper.

'For a beginner you're very good. That's because you

like cock and enjoy giving. I'm going to make you love it more and want me always. And I'm going to create an erotic world for us to dwell in, more exciting than anything you can imagine.'

'Promise?' was her only reply, and they both burst into gleeful laughter. And Gideon loved her that little bit more because they could laugh together in their lust.

It was thrilling for him as he fed himself slowly into her mouth and down to the very back of her throat, feeling her take him over as he fucked and she instinctively used her tongue and sucked. He held back from coming and satisfying himself because he wanted her to share in that first exquisite orgasm they were to have together.

He swept her into his arms and they fell on to the bed. 'Trust me, and I'll make you the happiest woman in the world,' he told her.

He unclipped the garter belt and tossed it across the room. Then, going between her now spread legs, he raised her off the bed and looked hungrily at her cunt. He caressed it, spread open her labia and licked the soft pink flesh beneath while fingering her clitoris and teasing the opening to her most secret soul.

Dendre had to bite into the flesh on the back of her hand to keep herself from screaming, so intense was her pleasure. She burned hot as a flame for her lover. She clawed at his shoulders and felt herself contracting her cunt, wriggling her pelvis. She was more alive than she had ever been in her life. All thought vanished from her mind. She wanted more, much more, to reach greater heights of passion that she now knew she had. At a glance he saw her caress her breasts, pinch her nipples, tear at her own flesh. It was thrilling for him to see how she burned for him.

Gideon liked loving her, enjoyed bringing her out of

repressed lust and into the open. It excited him to set her free to enjoy her sexuality. In full command of her now, he slipped on top of Dendre while flagrantly continuing pleasuring her in cunnilingus. They assumed a position that gave them both intense oral bliss, where Dendre could caress his muscular bottom and back. They discovered an intimacy where all thought, all the world outside sex, was left behind as they soared to heights of erotic bliss.

Several hours later she lay in her lover's arms, ashamed for having given herself so easily to Gideon, worried what he might think of her, embarrassed by the amount of sexual pleasure she'd derived from sex with a man she had only known for an hour. She felt anxious because he had changed her from the person she had been into a woman who was a stranger to her.

As for Gideon: he had never bargained on her being a virgin. He neither liked deflowering a woman nor having sex with one who knew nothing about erotic feelings or how to satisfy a man. But Dendre had turned out to be an exception to this. What she lacked in experience, she made up for in her appreciation of sexuality. Her skittishness about it, the fear and surprise that shone from time to time in her eyes, her sincerity, caused him to understand he was the first man she had ever been with and somehow he loved her more for that and was tender and loving when he penetrated her. He had caused her that most exquisite, frightening, yet thrilling moment of pain most virgins experience but had followed it with hours of pleasure that only great fucking can give.

Gideon had dozed off several times during their afternoon of love making. Now awake, he turned on his side to face her. She had draped a sheet over her and was lying quite still, looking vacantly up at the ceiling. There seemed no anxiety but maybe a tinge of remorse for something of herself lost forever. He kissed her on the cheek and stroked her hair and she turned her head so she could look at him.

'You're very quiet,' he told her.

'I don't know quite what to say. I think I'm overwhelmed by you, what we have been together. I'm in awe of that.'

'I know. Do you want to talk about it?' he asked as he toyed with her hair and slowly removed the sheet from her body. She made an attempt to cover herself with it again but it was useless. He slid it slowly, teasingly, off her.

'You mean the fucking, not *that*. You're a big girl now, Dendre Moscowitz. You can say fuck. And, by the way, you were very good at it. Delicious, in fact,' he told her.

'I never knew I was capable of enjoying such sexual decadence,' she told him, a slight smile on her lips.

Gideon began to laugh. 'That's better! But, darling Dendre, going down on a man or a man going down on a woman, sodomy, your riding my cock, my fucking you into oblivion, you running with the sweet nectar of orgasm, both yours and mine, is hardly decadence, just sex. Decadence, depravity, debauchery . . . not for our first erotic encounter. We'll have a lifetime together to share those passions.'

Dendre's heart fluttered at his words 'a lifetime together'. He loved her, meant to marry her! She flung herself against him and kissed him all over his face. Her eyes filled with tears of happiness. He eased her away from him and arranged her body in a sensationally wanton position. Her hair looked wild and sexy on the pillow. He positioned the angle of her head then draped the blood-stained sheet so that it lay just barely under her bottom and protruded seductively between her provocatively open legs, draped over one thigh, the corner of it culminating in her hand. He suggested she think of him fucking her, of her coming, and that she should use her imagination to bring herself to orgasm so that she

58

might experience that delicious moment of bliss while he painted her.

'I think you are magnificent and we should capture you on canvas, for us and for posterity. Men and women alike will adore looking at you, be thrilled by where you are, who you are, in my portraits. They will yearn for the erotic promise blooming before them.' With that he ran naked through the studio to collect a huge sheet of paper and sticks of charcoal.

'Gideon, promise me no one will see these drawings?'

'Don't be ridiculous! One day people will line up in museums to see the drawings, the paintings, the water-colours, I will do of you. They will pay millions of dollars to possess you in oils, as I have had you in the flesh.'

'Maybe one day, but for now it's important to me that what's happened between us remains personal, for our eyes only. It's too intimate. I would die of shame if anyone but you and me saw them.'

Dendre had brought Gideon immense pleasure from when he'd first spotted her sitting alone on the park bench. He felt differently about her than he did most women he bedded. It was the purity of the love she felt for him. He had never experienced love and generosity, sacrifice of self for him and him alone. Once tasted it become an aphrodisiac for him. He wanted more, her kind of love, just for him, and all the time. She nourished all his senses. She would be a joy to mould into a muse, furnish his erotic fantasies and life as a painter. And he would raise her up always that little bit more, for herself. She would love him until death. He was as sure of that as he was that the sun would rise again the next day.

Looking wanton, as erotic and depraved as any woman in love who wants to please her man, Gideon was aware of the sacrifice Dendre was making but he was not a man who appreciated martyrdom.

He sat down next to her and caressed her breasts, kissed her sweetly on the mouth. Not angrily, in fact quite tenderly, he told her, 'I could never promise you that. I'm an artist, I don't paint for my work not to be seen. That's an unreasonable demand. Either you want to pose for me or you don't. If we are to stay together, you have to give me everything from the heart, with no strings attached, or don't give it at all. That's how I'll love you, what I'll expect from you. If the time comes that you can't do that, fair enough. We'll go our separate ways. My work is my life, everything else comes after that. You have to think about that, whether or not you can live for my work, for me.

'In defence of myself and how I want to live, I can promise you only one thing. One day the rewards will be immense, and if we are still together then we'll have lived our lives to the fullest, have the world at our feet.'

Chapter 5

Gideon and Dendre were walking arm in arm towards the entrance of the nearest subway station. Occasionally he would stop to take her in his arms and kiss her lovingly. Like a bolt of lightning they had been struck by unexpected love and were, in their own individual ways, quite dazed by what had happened to them.

'When will I see you again?' he asked as he toyed with the narrow lapels of her coat.

'I keep imagining I'll wake up and today, you, what we have had together, will all have been a dream. See you again? I don't even want to leave you,' she told him.

'Then don't,' he answered.

'If only you meant that,' she replied, and bit her bottom lip nervously.

'I never say anything I don't mean, Dendre.'

'I should have been home two hours ago, my mother will be frantic. I have to go. I don't think you understand – this is the most important and thrilling afternoon of my life. I've fallen in love with you, Gideon, and I need to come to terms with that. I'm a simple Jewish girl from Brooklyn who in her whole life has never expected or wanted to be anything other than that. And then you come along and turn my head and my heart around.'

'Stay the night with me.'

'I can't. What would I tell my mother?'

'I can't believe you said that! You tell her everything, like some pathetic teenager? Mamma approval, Dada love. There has to be a beloved elder brother too. You live and think like a bourgeois, my dear, but you fuck and love the erotic like a libertine. Straddle both lives and you'll have the best of everything. That's what I want for you, to be happy.'

What was he telling her? There was sarcasm in his voice but no disdain. There was too a hint of indifference as to whether she did stay the night with him and that frightened her. What if she lost him! The thought was unbearable. Tears came to her eyes.

'Tomorrow. I'll come to you after classes tomorrow.'

'Why not tonight?' he insisted.

'I've never spent the night with a man. Try and understand, I have a family to answer to. We're close-knit, everything to each other, and I simply can't run away from that. I need some time to ease myself away from them, but I don't want to make a mistake and lose you.'

They were standing at the entrance to the subway, Dendre looking wretched with anguish. He felt pity for her lack of courage, certainly not anger. It surprised him that he respected her because she wanted to do what was right for all concerned. He knew that if this was the stand she would take about her family obligations then she would take no less a one for him. Instinctively he knew she was the woman for him to marry, with whom to build a life and career. She was a solid foundation on which to place his ladder. With Dendre Moscowitz as his bedrock he could climb, rung by rung, through the art world to the top where he expected to reign supreme.

'You won't lose me. Tomorrow then, whenever it suits you,' he told her with a smile.

'You're not angry?' she asked

'I'm never angry. If I don't like what's around me, I simply leave. Stop worrying, stop fidgeting. It's never attractive. This has been a great day. Now I'm going back to the studio to work and you're going home.'

They kissed and Gideon watched her descend the stairs and be swallowed up by the stream of people making their way uptown for the evening. She took only a few steps before she turned for one last look at him but he was already gone.

There were crowds of people waiting on the platform and Dendre distracted herself trying to work out where they had all come from since she hardly remembered seeing a soul on the way from Gideon's to the subway station. That dead silence that happens at stations was suddenly broken by a loud swish of wind coming through the tunnel followed by the bright light from a train, the rattle of metal on the tracks. The train screeched to a halt, and with a hissing sound and the sliding back of the doors, the train had arrived. Walking through the near-empty car, Dendre took a seat between a black man dozing and a turbanned Indian reading a paperback book: *Business Success in 80 Days*.

She swayed to the rhythm of the wobbling carriage as it sped under the city's streets. For several minutes Dendre was mesmerised by the sight of people standing rigid, as if suspended from the leather straps and looped handles they used for support against the rock and roll of the underground train as it barrelled at high speed through the tunnel. Some read newspapers under the bright lights, others stared into space. She was used to riding the subway, changing from one train to another several times during the long ride back to Brooklyn. Here was familiar territory she could relate to. This was her world, the place where she felt secure. Where she had been with Gideon was foreign territory, but once

63

experienced she knew she would rather die than leave it. She felt that no sacrifice would be too great to make for being loved by Gideon. She felt suddenly ecstatic, understood now what he meant when he told her he wanted her to be happy and that would mean her straddling two worlds, his and hers. He was right of course, and that was exactly what she intended to do. How clever he is, she told herself, and leaned back and closed her eyes. It was all set. She knew where she was going. They would be together all the days of their lives.

Dendre had changed trains for the last time. Once settled, she tried to relive her day with Gideon but couldn't conjure it up. All that came were thoughts of her mother, father, brother. Gideon had of course been right about that too; there was an elder brother, Orlando, who adored her. Of course she could never tell them about Gideon, about losing her virginity and loving every minute of it. She would have to squirrel her happiness away and take it from its hiding place only when she was alone in her room, until slowly and carefully she was able to introduce Gideon to the family.

The Moscowitz house was not stylish: small, cream-painted, square in shape with a porch large enough to hold a wooden slatted swing hanging on chains, black shutters and window boxes with dead plants in them. It was flanked, more or less, by carbon copies the whole length of both sides of the street. There was, however, a large tree in the overgrown yard at the back and a small patch of lawn with more bald patches than grass in the front. No, the Moscowitzes were certainly not stylish.

It was dark out and the porch light was on. Dendre put the key in the lock and pushed the door open. She was greeted by the delicious scent of her mother's cooking: sweet and sour stuffed cabbage, roast beef, potato dumplings. The aroma and atmosphere of comfort and love blocked thoughts of Gideon and her lecherous afternoon from her mind.

It was only when the family didn't rush forward in a panic to greet her that Dendre realised this was one of the three nights she usually spent studying art in Manhattan at Cooper Union. Instead her father greeted her with a kiss and took her coat. Dendre loved him as did most people who knew him. He and Orlando, her brother, were the men in her life, the only ones she had ever truly cared about. Now that she had met Gideon she had someone to measure them against. And compared to the vital, handsome, inspiring man she had fallen in love with, her father looked old, tired and worn out. That wrenched her heart. She flung her arms around his neck, gave him a hug and clung to him for several seconds.

Possibly for the first time Dendre saw him as he really was, without that thing daughters have of making their fathers their hero, the white knight always ready to ride up and save them. Hershel Moscowitz was a master furrier, a meek man without dreams, happy with his lot in life. He was a man dedicated to peace at any price, happy in the security of his religion and otherwise unambitious life. Dendre's mother, Frieda, quietly dominated the household. Both her parents were book lovers, readers and voyeurs, rather than doers. Of the two it was Frieda who lived vicariously through novels, hence her children's names, Dendre and Orlando, found in two blockbusters consumed on the annual week's summer holiday in the Catskill Mountains, Upper State New York.

Dendre's mind was reeling as she stepped away from her father. 'How was school today?' he asked. 'And the art class, Baby? You had a good day, I hope?'

Fortunately, Dendre was left with no time to answer because her mother arrived, saying, 'Schel, every night she comes home, you ask her the same questions. How interesting a day can Dendre have at New York University studying bookkeeping? Bookkeeping is bookkeeping.' It was not said unkindly, more matter-of-factly, and Frieda, who clearly adored her husband, stroked his cheek and smiled as she spoke.

'You're right, of course,' he answered meekly.

'Supper in twenty minutes, you two,' announced Frieda, and placing her arm around Dendre's shoulders walked with her daughter to the foot of the stairs, giving her a hug before turning away to return to the kitchen.

Dendre started up the stairs, stopped and sat down in the middle. This house and her parents' love and respect for her wrapped themselves round her like the softest cashmere blanket. Dendre hugged herself. Her mother and father gave each other every support. Were she and Gideon capable of such love and devotion? Were they as capable of making enormous sacrifices for their children as Frieda and Herschel had made for theirs? All the family and her parents' friends admired the Moscowitzes because of the life they lived: simple, stress-free, loving. Dendre realised that she had never heard a cross word in this house. Hard times (and there had been many), better times, they never complained, merely lived them out the best they could.

The family – aunts, uncles, cousins – all much better off, financially and socially, claimed that it was Frieda's love for her husband, her devotion to his and their children's needs, her selfish selflessness, that had kept the family as *she* wanted it. A pointless criticism since they had no proof that her husband and children were anything but happy and well adjusted for it.

A wave of anxiety swept over Dendre. She and her family lived in the bosom of middle-class morality. Theirs was a staid and boring life and they were content with it. Even now Dendre enjoyed being who and what she was, felt pride in her roots, though Gideon had seduced her away from them and showed her another way to live and love; above all to have a dream and follow it. She felt there was no turning back to her loving parents whose influence had kept her in the heart of the Jewish community which until now had always been the foundation of her life. To do that would be to give up Gideon and that was an impossibility. She wanted him to love her always as he had done that afternoon, again and again, forever. His passion had burned her deep, marked her as his for life. She was his as she could never be another man's.

She heard her mother humming in the kitchen and under-stood that she was indeed Frieda's daughter; she could love Gideon on a grand scale as her mother loved her father. As for Gideon, there was nothing of her father in him. Gideon would love her the best way he could and that would have to be enough for her. Dendre made a pact with herself that she would abide by this. That seemed to galvanise her. She sprang up from the stairs, taking the remainder two at a time, and went not to her room but to knock on Orlando's door and walk straight in.

Her brother looked up from the book he was reading. How handsome, bright, sweet and kind he looked to Dendre. She went to sit on the bed next to him. Orlando was the pride of the family, being in his last year at Harvard medical school.

'Hi,' she said.

'Hi, yourself,' he answered, a broad smile crossing his face.

Dendre noted that her brother always had a smile for her. He adored her. Being five years older than Dendre, he had felt protective of her ever since she was a baby. It was he who as a child had called her 'Baby' until it stuck and became her nickname. Dendre admired her brother. He was at Harvard on scholarships and worked two jobs as well to keep himself there. Herschel Moscowitz simply did not have the money to send a son through Harvard.

Now, having experienced sex and the thrill of orgasm for the first time, Dendre could understand why women ran after her brother. He had a sexuality about him that, combined with his self-assurance and good looks, was very exciting. How odd, she thought, suddenly to think of Orlando in a sexual context. She sensed that he would understand her passion for Gideon, and strangely would not be shocked by her choice.

'When do you have to be back at school, Orlando?' she asked.

'Day after tomorrow.'

'I've met someone. The man I'm going to marry. I think you'll like him.'

'Baby!'

'I want to tell you about him – us. I want you to meet him. We'll come and see you off at Grand Central.'

'Do Mom and Dad know about this?'

'No, and they mustn't, not for a while yet. They have to get to know him first.'

'He's not Jewish?'

'No, I don't know what he is.'

'Marry out of the faith and it'll kill Dad, shock the family. Maybe you'd better tell me all about this great love? From the beginning.'

And so Dendre did tell her brother everything about her meeting with Gideon and falling in love with him. Though she admitted that she had gone to bed with him, she was careful to skirt around the details, feeling some embarrassment over discussing sex with her brother. The more Orlando heard, the more upset he was. He rose from the bed and walked around the room. His heart nearly broke for her when she told him that she loved Gideon beyond reason, beyond life itself. He went to her when she started sobbing.

'Why are you crying, Baby?' asked Orlando as he sat her down and placed his arm round her shoulders. She leaned against him.

'Not from grief or despair but because I had no idea what it was to love as I do now. I've never felt as good as this in my whole life.'

'Baby, are you sure this isn't just sexual infatuation? Every woman falls in love with the first man they have sex with, and most especially if that first experience is a good one. By all accounts yours was and I like the guy already for that. A new world has opened up for you. You're a woman now, not a baby. We'll have to treat you accordingly, maybe even stop calling you Baby.'

'Oh, would you, Orlando? Gideon would hate my being called Baby,' she told her brother.

'Hey, wait a minute, Dendre. You've had one experience with this guy, known him for less than twenty-four hours, and already you're concerned about what he thinks and feels? I think you've had too much, too soon with this guy. Give him some space to think about you and come after you.'

'I'm seeing him tomorrow. We love each other, Orlando, in just the same way. Be happy for us,' she pleaded as her eyes filled with tears. There was a tremor in her voice.

He took a clean handkerchief from his pocket and handed it to her. 'Baby, you're such an innocent. Men don't love women the way women want them to. They love women the best way they can, on their terms.'

'Gideon has already told me that and it's fine with me.'

'And who's going to handle Mom and Dad? I'm off tomorrow, remember. Put him off for a few weeks, give yourself some time, and don't do anything rash is what I suggest.'

'I can't do that.'

'Why not, for God's sake?'

'Because I'll lose him. You don't understand how remarkable he is, Orlando. He's already my life.'

'This is crazy!' he told her.

Their conversation was interrupted by their mother at the foot of the stairs, shouting, 'Dinner's on the table, you two.'

Brother and sister rose from the bed together, looking at one another, not quite knowing what to do. This was not a family that kept secrets. Orlando opened his arms and Dendre ran into them, tears running down her cheeks. He would help her. He simply loved his sister too much not to.

Frieda Moscowitz was not the sort of woman who could talk of intimate things easily. She was a pots and pans home builder, a nourisher of her husband and children. Sex was a foreign language as far as she was concerned and so she was unable to talk to her daughter about it. Frieda assumed that the husband she would find for her would take on that job. It would be they, after all, who would be doing it together. Sex embarrassed her.

At the dinner table the four of them spoke about mundane things: local gossip, a cousin's indiscretions. The meal nearly over, Orlando looked across the table at Dendre and made a signal suggesting she should speak up about Gideon. Several minutes passed before she said, 'I met a man today – an artist, a poor and unknown painter who will one day be very famous.'

'That's nice, dear,' said her mother as she rose from her chair to clear the dishes.

Silence fell heavily on the table. Orlando raised an eyebrow. When Frieda returned with a mould of orange-and-lime Jello piled high with strawberries in the centre of the ring, all Dendre could think of was how she detested her mother's Jello. It was semi-hard, rubbery and tasteless. Gideon must never be served any. She made a mental note to be a better cook than her mother.

'I would like to bring him home for dinner,' announced Dendre.

Everyone at the table looked at her but it was her father who said, 'Why? You never bring people we don't know home for a meal.'

'I want you all to meet him. He's special and likes Mamma's cooking. I shared my lunch with him today.'

'Is he from Brooklyn?' asked her mother.

'No, Mother,' answered Orlando.

The Moscowitz family believed the world began and ended in Brooklyn, like so many families born and bred in that borough. The wider world was conceived as a marvellous adventure but a foreign place, whether it be Manhattan, just across the East River, Boston or Paris. Therefore a look of concern passed between Frieda and Herschel.

'So where is he from, Dendre, and how is it you know so much about this boy, Orlando?' asked Frieda.

'St Louis,' she answered.

'I've never met anyone who came from St Louis,' said Herschel, chasing his bouncing Jello round his plate.

'Neither have I, Dad. And, Mom, he's not a boy,' answered Dendre.

'Oh,' remarked Frieda, then stopped asking questions. Orlando knew his mother well. She was out of her depth with

71

strangers or anything that intruded on her domain. Now she would retreat into silence. One thing about Frieda: she knew when she was beaten and always stepped back gracefully. It had been the tone of her daughter's voice that had signalled that retreat. Herschel looked disturbed but said nothing.

The following day at college was torture for Dendre. She could think of nothing but Gideon and resented every minute spent away from him. Was it a dream? Wishful thinking? Had it really happened at all? Had it only been yesterday that a sexual life had opened to her? The hours seemed to drag by and then her last class was over and she rushed away to be with Gideon.

Her knees were weak as she pressed the button on the intercom and the door automatically unlocked. She trembled with anticipation and questions kept flashing through her head. Why had he not spoken through the intercom, was he expecting someone else, was he angry because she had not stayed the night? She pushed the door open and entered the hall. Her eyesight was just adjusting to the darkness when the lights were turned on. She gasped and placed her hand over her heart.

'It's about time. I was beginning to think you weren't coming,' announced Gideon from the top of the stairs.

All was right with the world. He still wanted her. How handsome he looked as he rushed down the stairs to sweep her into his arms. He kissed her lavishly on her face. Dendre began tearing at her clothes, wanting to be naked in his arms.

'Tell me you love me?' she begged.

'I love you,' he answered.

'And you'll never let me go away from you again?' she pressed.

'I'll never let you go again,' he repeated. 'And those are not just words, Dendre, they're intentions. I worked all through the night, look.'

Gideon placed her gently on her feet and, hand in hand, they walked up the stairs and then along the length of his studio. Dendre was astounded: huge drawings of her were pinned to the walls, some with splashes of colour. The red droplets of virgin blood were on one; red lips and fingernails and toenails on another. Others were in sepia and black. Most of the portraits were life-size; others were detailed studies of various parts of her anatomy. They were all astonishingly vibrant and raunchy. The emotion came through in her eyes: a hunger for sex, a body bursting with lasciviousness. Her sexuality seduced the viewer, embraced him as he had never been embraced before. Was this how Gideon saw her? Had she inspired him to paint so masterfully? He had translated her into a vision that would stir the coldest heart. What nineteen-year-old would not be flattered by his genius and lay down her life for the love of such a man? Dendre was thrilled by his work and threw herself into his arms.

'They're marvellous! I feel faint with excitement.'

Gideon threw back his head and laughed. 'And so you should,' he told her.

A moment of silence fell between them that only enhanced the sexual longing they had for each other. Love and lust together, the most potent of drugs, intoxicated them. For Dendre this second experience of intercourse was even more thrilling than her first. Portraits of herself everywhere beamed down at her and their debauchery only served to excite her further. She heard herself asking Gideon to do things to her she had never even heard of. Where did all that come from – a will to be possessed utterly by him, to show him her desire to submit to anything for another climax with him, and another and another? She wanted to die and be reborn again and again in his arms in sexual bliss, and Gideon adored her for that. When, on their knees, Gideon behind her, he moved between both her willing orifices, Dendre felt as if she were losing her senses, so acute was the bliss of being so completely filled by him. She called out, screamed her pain and her pleasure.

Her hunger for sex to the extreme fired Gideon's imagination and he whispered to her, never changing the rhythm of his fucking, all the erotic things they would do together.

When they were replete they fell asleep in each other's arms on the bare boards in the middle of the studio. On waking, the scent of sex, the aroma of lust, still clung to them. Dendre wanted to lick her lover awake, to hold on to that scent they had created together, breathe it deep into her lungs. Where had the world gone, her family, her middle-class morality that told her she was behaving like a slut? Only Gideon really mattered to her now.

After lying on her side so that she might look at her handsome lover, feeling incredibly grateful that he should take on such a plain girl to love, she licked Gideon awake then proceeded to dress. He watched her slip one of her stockings up her leg then took the second from her hand and drew it carefully over the other. He kissed her knee and smiled.

There was something more in that smile than he had ever shown her before: a wealth of generosity, warmth, promise. With extraordinary tenderness he helped her from the floor and dressed her. For Dendre it was the final act that would cleave her to him until the day she died.

Chapter 6

Gideon was ten years older than Dendre, a man experienced in life. His world was big, wide and dangerous and that would frighten her mother and father. His not being of their faith would make him unacceptable as a husband for their only daughter. Those were the things going through her mind while she watched him dress.

'I told my brother about you,' she blurted out.

Gideon was just slipping his jumper on over his head. He hesitated then said, 'Not revelations about our sex life, I bet?'

He saw the rush of blood appear in her cheeks and realised he was embarrassing her. Gideon went to her, took her in his arms and told her, 'That was not said to embarrass you. It was actually meant to be a joke. What did you tell him?'

'That we are in love and I'm going to marry you,' she told him rather boldly.

He was amused and a smile broke across his face. 'You're quite sure of that, are you?'

'You will never find a better wife. No woman will love you more than I will, and you know that. That's why you'll marry me. And for love, of course.'

This young and naive woman who was so pliable in his hands was right. Gideon liked her that little bit more because she was speaking the truth. He raised both her hands to his

75

lips and kissed her fingers, then told her, 'You don't know me. Marriage to me will not be an easy life for you. My work will always come before anything else, that and my freedom. We'll be poor and you will have to work to keep us alive, at least until I'm discovered. But one day we will have it all: success, money, an exciting and adventurous life. Are you certain you love me enough to live like that? Oh, and one other thing – I'm a benevolent tyrant but a tyrant nevertheless.'

'I'm Brooklyn, Jewish, family-minded, with a middle-class morality that knows nothing else. That's what I will bring into this marriage, can *you* live with that?' she asked him with metal in her voice.

There it was again, forthright honesty, a rod of steel for a spine, still a virgin in so many ways. Gideon quite thrilled at the idea of a lifetime of seducing Dendre into his world while dwelling in comfort in hers, the hearth and the home, a love he had yearned for since childhood and until now never received.

There could be but one answer. 'When do you take me home for dinner?' he asked with a twinkle in his eyes and a smile on his lips.

'Tonight?' she suggested, the happiness in her voice ringing like church bells.

'Let's go, I'm famished,' was his reply.

'I have to call my mother and tell her you're coming. It's only polite,' she told him.

'We can call from the bar round the corner,' he suggested.

'Gideon, my brother is waiting for us at the Angel. We can all ride home together.'

'Oh, I see. He's here to vet me?'

Dendre felt some embarrassment. 'I was going to ask you

to meet him over a drink? Please don't be angry, but he wants to see what you're like. He goes back to Harvard tomorrow and is anxious that I might be getting involved with the wrong man. You really can't blame him for caring about me.'

'No, I can't, but he'll have to pick up the tab. I have no money to pay for drinks at the Angel.'

Orlando was sitting at a table reading a book. Every time the door opened his eyes shifted from the page. So many people came and went the waiting was beginning to grate on his nerves. He had agreed to wait until five o'clock. It was five-thirty when he looked up from his book again, telling himself, This is the last time. No Dendre and I'm going home.

But it was Dendre and her man and they looked so happy, so full of the joys of love, it brought Orlando to his feet to wave to them. Even before they reached his table and Gideon had said a word, Orlando was impressed by the man, seduced by his charisma. Gideon Palenberg had about him an aura of greatness, something that separated him from other men. It was there in every step he took, his sureness, power, the sexuality that could turn any woman's head, the intelligence in that handsome face. Orlando could understand why Dendre had fallen so heavily in love with this man but his heart sank for his sister. Love her as he did, he was a realist. She had taken on greatness but could she rise to it? What he did know was that she had found a man in a million and she was right not to let him go.

Introductions were made and the two men shook hands. 'I'd like to see your paintings,' were the first words Orlando said to Gideon.

'Easily done, come along.'

'You might be shocked,' offered Dendre.

'They're portraits of your sister, the best work I have ever done. And if you appreciate art, you'll be thrilled by them, not shocked.'

'Then let's go,' said Orlando.

Dendre made her phone call to her mother. The two men talked to each other easily while they waited for her return. Gideon found Orlando intelligent, sensitive, and knowledgeable about art. He was fascinated to learn that the Moscowitzes were in their own simple way a cultured family and that Orlando and the family had taken advantage of Brooklyn's museums, concert halls and libraries where most families only watched TV for entertainment.

In the studio, Orlando was indeed thrilled but shocked as well. Who was this woman in the portraits? The other side of Dendre. Surely not Baby whom he had loved and thought he knew?

'They're magnificent, very exciting, Gideon. They're great paintings,' Orlando commented. And then the two men talked art and great artists.

The three of them were sitting on the bed, discussing which drawing Orlando would like to have. 'I can't accept such a valuable gift, Gideon. One day it will be worth a fortune,' he protested.

'I know. I'm usually very mean about giving my work away, but I really want you to have it. I am, after all, taking something away from you and your family that is far more precious.'

Dendre thought that her heart would burst with love for Gideon. He considered her more precious than his work! Her brother already liked him, was indeed in some awe of Gideon. That was all the approval she really needed. It would be easy to win her mother and father over with Orlando on her side.

Gideon was appalled at the amount of time it took to ride

the subway to Brooklyn and decided never to make the trip there again in this manner. The journey alone convinced him there would be no Manhattan-Brooklyn courtship. It would have to be marriage, as soon as possible.

Orlando used his key and the three of them entered the house. Herschel Moscowitz poured them all whisky, but no Frieda appeared. Gideon liked Herschel immediately, sensing Dendre's father had a creative soul that had died a long, drawn-out death long ago. Life had beaten him but what remained was a loving, uncomplicated man who lived one day at a time.

'You're a painter, my daughter tells me?'

'Yes, I am, and what do you do for a living, Mr Moscowitz?' asked Gideon.

'I'm a furrier.'

'In what he does, my father is an artist in his own right,' said Dendre.

Somehow Gideon was certain that was true. Herschel raised his glass and said, *'L'chaim,'* as a toast before he swigged his drink down in one. He then announced to Gideon, 'That means "to life" in Yiddish. We're Jewish. And you?'

'Well, I'm not Jewish.'

'That's all right so long as you're a human being,' said Herschel.

'I'll go get Mother,' said Orlando.

'No, let me. Just point me to the kitchen,' said Gideon.

He had never felt so comfortable and safe as he did in that lacklustre, somewhat shabby house with its aroma of roasting chicken, cinnamon and vanilla, and in the bosom of Dendre and her family. He had never met people like this, so simple and honest. Their kindness and lack of guile clung to them like a heady perfume.

On entering the kitchen Gideon came face to face with Frieda who was ladling chicken soup from a pot into a tureen. They gazed at each other for several seconds before she continued with her task.

'I know I'm a last-minute guest but I'm a grateful one. You see, I already like your cooking,' said Gideon, walking across the room to kiss her on the cheek.

Frieda was still recovering from having an uninvited if handsome stranger in her kitchen when he gave her that peck on the cheek. She felt his dynamic charm, something more than she had ever experienced before. Frieda knew instantly he was the one in the million everyone hopes to meet sometime in their lives. She could well understand why Dendre had brought him home to dinner.

'How long have you known my daughter?' she asked.

'A little more than a day but it feels like a lifetime,' he replied.

'You're a fast worker, Mr . . .'

'Gideon Palenberg is my name. And yours?'

'Palenberg,' she repeated, and did not offer hers.

'You must call me Gideon, and what shall I call you? Surely not Mrs Moscowitz – too formal,' he told her.

She hesitated over using his Christian name but finally managed it. 'My name is Frieda, Gideon,' she told him.

She placed the lid on the tureen and went to the cooker to remove a pan of steamed dumplings. She placed one of the large fluffy dumplings on a saucer and handed it to Gideon along with a fork. She was captivated by him, though she sensed a power in him that was too wild and free for her liking. He was all the things Herschel had never been, that Dendre was not, and that frightened her. What did he want from her daughter when he could have most any woman he wanted? A stranger had invaded her house and none of the family would ever be the same afterwards. That, finally, was what worried her most.

'Frieda, this is delicious,' he remarked.

'Gideon, you like my cooking, but how much do you like my daughter? Clearly enough to drag yourself out here to Flatbush for a meal. That worries me. An innocent girl involved with such a charming and handsome man worries me even more. A cook I may be but I'm no gourmet chef and by your looks and manner it's not ethnic food you're used to and crave. You wouldn't take advantage of a girl like Dendre, would you?' she asked.

'Your mothering is showing, Frieda. I like that, it's something I have missed all my life. I'll not lie to you. Since you're being so direct with me, I will be with you. Yes, I have taken advantage of your daughter, and tonight after dinner I'm going to take her home with me and take advantage of her again. And for the rest of her life I hope she will do the same with me. We fell in love. One, two looks at each other and we knew. Frieda, I want to marry Dendre and will feel proud and blessed to have you, Herschel and Orlando as family.'

Frieda turned the colour of ashes and a dizziness came over her. She stretched out her arms to steady herself and Gideon went to her aid and took her in his arms, holding her close to him. He tried to comfort her.

'She's only a child, Gideon,' she managed.

'Not so, Frieda. She is very much a woman – warm, sweet, kind, without malice. Just like her mother. We love each other, Frieda, and are willing to struggle through life together. Be happy for us, come along with us. I promise you'll not be sorry. I may not be the husband you visualised for her but I am the one she has chosen.'

All his life Gideon was able to bend people to feed his ego, his libido, his art. Kindness, generosity, affability, are as intriguing as arrogance and it was all of those things that finally won over the Moscowitz family.

He swept Dendre away from them on that one and only time he visited Brooklyn, leaving the three others reeling from his visit and the loss of Dendre to a stranger. It had been too fast, too unthinkable for Herschel to handle, and when he kissed his daughter farewell it was he who broke down in tears.

While unpacking the few things she had brought to her new home, Dendre was thinking about that and what Gideon had said to her father. 'Herschel, I know you're hurting, but try and remember I'm not stealing your daughter away from you. Our door will always be open to you, our hearts, our very souls. I'm marrying you and Frieda and Orlando as much as I am marrying Dendre.'

Gideon could not have said anything nicer, more generous. It eased the shock of having the family suddenly turned upside down. For that they were grateful to him.

In bed, enfolded in each other's arms, Dendre told him, 'You were marvellous with my parents and brother.'

'That was easy because I liked them enormously. Are you happy to be in your new home with me?' he asked as he fondled her breasts and kissed her stomach.

'Blissfully happy,' she told him as she slid on top of his body and kissed him. She knew better than to enquire about his own family. She had tried once and Gideon had made it plain he would not discuss them other than to say he had been raised by his aunt.

Aunt Martha remained a mystery to Dendre. Gideon rarely spoke about her. When she'd asked him about his aunt, Gideon had politely but firmly told her, 'I'd rather we didn't talk about her.'

Ten days after they met they were married. And in those ten days the pattern of Dendre's life with Gideon was established. She began to know him as he had described himself to her. He was indeed a benevolent tyrant but he was besides decidedly in love with her and to have him loving her was all. Nothing else in her life seemed to matter but Gideon and his work.

As hard a life as it was for them, Dendre adored living as a poor, undiscovered artist's wife. She still went to school but quit her night classes at Cooper Union and took a waitressing job in a coffee shop in the Village. Both she and Gideon thrived on their difficult circumstances. Every week they would pool their money then allot the funds they needed for housekeeping. The remainder went on art materials.

If they were poor materially, they were wealthy in other ways. Their love for each other, their sexual life, his work, made up for the cold water and lack of heat in the studio. Gideon's work, his ego, his libido, his dreams, anything he desired, governed their lives – and that was just fine with Dendre. He was everything she wanted. Gideon was inspired, everything seemed to be working for him, and he was generous in his praise of his wife in the darkness of the night when he was making love to her.

Dendre relieved him of the mundane chores in life: shopping, cooking, keeping their living corner clean, paying the bills, so that he might paint. They survived on Frieda's food parcels that Dendre went to Brooklyn every week to collect. On rare occasions Frieda brought them to the studio. Those visits were infrequent because the poverty her daughter and son-in-law lived in upset her greatly. The few things she tried to give them to make their living corner look more like a home were rejected and she came to understand that offering them was wrong. They wanted nothing to clutter up their lives. In time she learned to appreciate the sacrifices Dendre and Gideon were making to live the way he dictated. Dendre's wages and a small cheque from his Aunt Martha, or the rare sale of a painting, kept them going.

About once a month Dendre's parents would arrive on a Sunday morning and Gideon would choose the exhibition he wanted to see in one of the museums. They would take the bus uptown, do the museum exhibition and then walk the streets of the Upper East Side, gazing into the closed art galleries. They would finally complete their day by eating huge sirloin steaks and baked potatoes dripping with butter in Joey George's Chop House on Lexington Avenue. They repeatedly talked about going to a different restaurant but never did. Herschel, who always picked up the tab, was a creature of habit.

Gideon loved the days when his parents-in-law arrived for their Sunday visit. He was extremely fond of Herschel and Frieda who, having been charmed by him and his belief in himself and his work, now supported him in any way they could. They were certain that one day they would be seeing his work in a museum.

The very first thing that Herschel would do upon arriving at the studio on one of their Sunday outings was to ask, 'You've been well, Dendre? You still happy with this genius you married?' and make an attempt to punch Gideon teasingly on the chin. Gideon would always duck and the two men would hug each other in greeting.

'Yes, Dad,' she would answer, and go to him for a kiss and a hug.

Invariably the next thing Herschel would say was, 'Gideon, let's have a look,' and he would show his father-in-law his latest work.

One evening after one of their Sunday outings, the fridge

and larder stocked by his parents-in-law, Gideon lay in bed
with Dendre and looked around his vast studio and the corner
he had designated their living space. How piteously poor they
were, yet Dendre had never complained. His parents-in-law
had reconciled themselves to accept her life as she wished to
live it with Gideon. How supportive they and his wife were
of his keeping his freedom and concentrating on his work.
Never a demand from Dendre. She always obeyed the ground
rules he had laid down before they were married, gave him
the firm foundation of love he had always hoped for and was
grateful to have. He had it all and was the happiest of men.
Taking stock of his life as it was now prompted Gideon to
speak to Dendre about his delight in their marriage.

'You do know, Dendre, that the reason this marriage is
working so well is not only because we love each other but
because we are so different and respect those differences.
We dip our toes into each other's lives and gain something
special from the experience.'

'You make it sound as if that's the way you want it to be
always?'

'I do. And it will be,' he replied.

Dendre felt the sting of fear. In the many hours when
Gideon was not with her, in those endless days and nights
when his work took over his life and she was forgotten, she
thought of him constantly, convincing herself that he did love
her as she wanted him to. Every hour of the day she yearned
for him. He took command of her life and she blossomed.
She fantasised that he loved her more than life itself. In time
she grew to believe that that particular fantasy was reality and
her passion for him became more intense. Fear of loss made
her devious: she went to great lengths never to let him know
how much more she wanted from him. She was stubborn and
proud, she wanted it to come from him voluntarily. However,

she would on occasion drop a word here or there that might lead him on to give more of himself to her.

In spite of her fear, she told him, 'Sometimes I think you married me for my family, you love them so.'

'I did, and I do,' he told her.

Dendre extricated herself from his arms and sat bolt upright. He sat up too and turned on the dim light they liked to have sex by. He was clearly amused.

'Do you love them more than me?' she asked point-blank.

'No, not more, as much as, but for different reasons,' he told her.

'I don't understand,' she said petulantly.

'No, I don't expect you do,' he said, tenderness in his voice.

This was the first time in all the months they had lived together that Dendre sensed a closeness between them that had not been brought about by their erotic couplings.

'Then tell me. I really need to know, Gideon.'

'Well, let me see,' he teased. Taking her in his arms and caressing her breasts, he continued, 'I love you for you yourself, because you're naive, good and kind, and extraordinarily sexy and good in bed. Because you're bright and timid but always rise to the occasion. You understand me and my work, are very bourgeois and give me everything I want.

'I love your family because they are good, kind, generous human beings, who recognise in me someone special who needs to be nourished with that Jewish love they are steeped in and I have been deprived of all my life. They, like you, are everything I am not nor do I wish to be.'

Gideon felt Dendre's body grow tense. Still in his arms, he turned her round to face him. 'Does that upset you?' he asked, rather surprised that such honesty might upset her.

Bravely she told him, 'You love us but you would not like

to be us. That's like giving a prize with the right hand and taking it away with the left.'

'Dendre, it's not in my nature to be like them. If you wanted a man like them then you picked the wrong one. We're together because I am something else and we add to each other's lives. I am the "significant other" in your life and it will always be that way.'

'Why should it be?' she pressed.

'Because we were born to be different people. Our formative years were spent poles apart and will have influenced who and what we are. You will always be in the bosom of your family, you are a replica of them, and I love you for it. I will always be the outsider, no matter how much fame and fortune and marital bliss I have. I have learned from childhood what it is to be an outsider and now I've grown into the role.'

'I think that's sad,' she said.

'Oh, my young, dear heart, you have a great deal of growing up to do and one day you'll understand that it's not sad to be different, an outsider, as long as you have faith in yourself and can walk that tight rope called life with chin up.

'I have always known that I was capable of love and passion on a grand scale but you are the only woman of the many I have had to whom I was able to express it. You're everything I have ever wanted: steeped in family love and loyalty, a woman willing to love me with unconditional surrender to my lust. One who is willing to share a life of poverty with me while I pursue my art, my dreams. You work for me, have become my provider, guard me from the outside world and any infringement that interferes with my work. I cherish you for that. I am constantly excited by you – your innocence. I adore opening up the world for you. You are a whore in bed which suits our sexual attraction to each other, or should I say needs? My constant seduction of you adds something thrilling to this game of love and marriage. Is the kind of love I have for you not enough?'

Gideon had once more seduced Dendre to him and she answered, 'More than enough. I love my life with you, Gideon. I want no other.'

For the first six months of their marriage Dendre and Gideon saw few people but Gideon's struggling painter friends and his wife's family. Gideon and his friends would visit each other's studios and look at each other's work. The men would talk art and share a meal. The women on their arms were young and for the most part street-smart, knowledgeable and very beautiful. Dendre was never quite able to make friends with any of them; they seemed to her too frivolous, too trendy. She watched Gideon's every move when there were other women around. He was the most attractive and vibrant man of their group and most women he met flirted with him.

Dendre learned to guard against their snatching her husband away from her. She listened and learned about art and the art world. She never stepped forward to express an opinion but instead clung to Gideon and played the role of loving wife to the hilt. The result was that she was thought to be dull, a middle-class moralist, a nonentity who belonged in the kitchen and the background of Gideon's life. The big question for the artists and their female companions was why he had married her.

They did not know that she did have opinions, and interesting ones, that she would discuss with Gideon. That he listened to her because she was clever and intelligent and mostly because she had the ability to be objective and honest. He was no fool, he could see in the eyes of his friends and most people they met that they simply could not understand his choice of wife. It was for that reason that when out in public he would be particularly affectionate to Dendre. It was also during that first year together that his work changed dramatically for the better. His friend, a dealer in Impressionist painting, Ben Borgnine, was certain this was the time for Gideon to show his work. He refused. Word went round the art world that the young painter Gideon Palenberg was something special. Dealers sent letters offering to look at his work. Dendre wrote polite replies which said in essence 'thank you, but no thank you. Maybe at a later date'.

She had now finished with college and had a problem getting a well-paid job so out of necessity she went freelance and was bookkeeper for several small shops on the Lower East Side. Thankfully one was a kosher delicatessen with a generous proprietor, and she rarely left the shop empty-handed. She kept her night waitressing job and in her spare time posed for Gideon. Life was hard for Dendre who sometimes felt she was always going to be living on leftovers from other people's lives.

There was a kind of hysteria in the art world at that time. The Abstract Expressionists were being challenged by Pop Artists. The dealers were searching for the next great art discovery. Letters from dealers and young museum directors trying to make a name for themselves arrived more frequently and still Gideon refused to show them his work.

Dendre, now eight months' pregnant and obsessed with her love for him, never asked him to reconsider. Instinctively she knew that Gideon would show his work at the right time and that when he did he would be a huge success.

Chapter 7

Some women bloom in pregnancy. Dendre did not. Her skin appeared sallow, her hair lost its lustre, her lips became puffy. But that did not matter to Gideon. He adored her even more during her pregnancy, had sex with her at every chance he could. She was heavy with child and carrying all in the front. Except for that her figure remained much the same. They had little time for anything but working and making love. These were the happiest days of Dendre's life.

Gideon was painting feverishly; he thrived on work and making love to Dendre. Their sex life was more adventurous. None of Gideon's erotic demands shocked or disturbed her. On the contrary, she was becoming obsessive about sex with Gideon and thought about it all the time. She was primed, ready and waiting, anywhere, anytime. She was enslaved by her lust and thought about sex and Gideon constantly. And that was just how he wanted her.

One night he woke Dendre and insisted she go with him to the centre of the studio where he had placed a chair. He invited her to sit down. He wanted her to be the first to see the exhibition he had been putting together for three years.

After she had taken her seat he told her, 'I'm ready to show. Tomorrow I will go uptown and invite three dealers to view this work, but I already know the one I want. Now feast your eyes.'

The studio was dimly lit except for spotlights shining against the empty white walls where on the floor leaning against them were his canvasses, facing the wall. Two large easels had been placed dramatically at angles from his exhibiting wall. Dendre sat in the chair wrapped in a woollen blanket, her heart racing. She could hardly think of the paintings, as anxious as she was to see them, because she realised that her life with Gideon, once the baby was born and he had his show, would change radically. She needed no further proof than to look at her husband. He had already set himself free from what had been. He was eager for tomorrow and all the days after that would take him where he wanted to go. She buried her anxiety at having to leave behind the simple and secluded life they had shared so happily.

Before he turned the first canvas round for viewing, Gideon went to Dendre and dropped to his knees in front of her. He opened the blanket she was huddled under and caressed the roundness of her swollen belly. He raised her nightdress and laid his head on her stomach, then kissed it and licked her flesh. He covered her again and wrapped her in the blanket once more. She was reassured by this gesture of love. They were both aware that this was the most intimate moment of their lives, nothing else would ever come close to it.

'I could never have done this without you, Dendre,' he told her.

Her heart swelled with love and pride because she knew that to be true. She would have liked him to kiss her on the lips and to tell her that he would love her always as he loved her now. But he didn't. Instead he rose from his knees and told her as he walked away from her, 'And so it begins.'

And so it did. The dealers came and they went and there were offers for a one-man show. Gideon, Dendre at his side, listened to the offers and played one dealer off against another.

Then a New York museum offered to take three paintings for their 'New Painters' exhibition. A Californian dealer flew into New York to see Gideon and offered to buy outright five of the canvasses. Gideon turned him down. He leaned heavily on Dendre's opinion on every little thing. Finally, after several weeks, Gideon got everything he wanted: a daughter whom they named Amber, the only dealer he really wanted to represent him – Haver Savage, a one-man show in New York of his oil paintings simultaneous with a one-man show of his water-colours and drawings in London.

Haver Savage was an important figure in the art world. Museums, critics, dealers and collectors listened to Haver. He managed only a few artists, the best Abstract Expressionists, and dealt in Picasso, Miro and Soutine. To have Haver for a dealer meant assured success.

A tall, needle-slender man, frighteningly urbane and handsome with the bluest eyes Dendre had ever seen, there was about him an air of sensual decadence that was fiercely attractive. He had wealth and power and knew how to use both. He was arrogant with a reputation for wasting no time on insignificant people.

The first occasion Dendre met him was when he arrived at the studio to view Gideon's paintings. He greeted her politely but spoke to Gideon quite differently. Dendre, standing next to her husband, sensed the empathy between the two men.

She kept wishing she had worn her best dress, had made up her face. This was the sort of man for whom those things mattered. Amber, lying in a padded Moses basket, was fast asleep in the corner they called home. Dendre prayed she wouldn't wake up and start crying. Domesticity would be viewed as a distraction by a man like Haver Savage, possibly enough to ruin this visit and Gideon's chances.

Her ears pricked up and she stopped thinking about herself

and how she appeared to Haver when she heard him say to her husband, 'We've missed you and your black coat with the velvet collar doing the gallery openings and art world parties, trying to make connections with the right collectors and dealers. I did wonder what had happened to you.'

The manner in which he said those things upset Dendre. She wanted to say, 'You make my husband sound like a hustler,' but kept silent and wondered instead why Gideon had never mentioned that part of his life. What more had he kept from her beside his troubled relationship with his Aunt Martha?

'Now you know, Haver. I married Dendre and have become the father of a beautiful baby girl called Amber. I've also had a breakthrough in my work and now I'm ready to show.'

The canvasses were all turned to the wall and two boys whom Gideon had picked up in the street and trained how to present his work for these exhibitions were standing by. He offered Haver the same chair set in the same place in the studio that Dendre and the other two dealers had occupied when they had had their own private views.

Haver sat down and told him, 'Before I see one painting I have to warn you that there is a less than one per cent chance I will take you on. I am only interested in new people if they excite my interest and I am so passionate about their work it would be impossible for me to let them go. I've taken on no one new for eight years now.'

'I don't have a problem with that, Haver. I want you for my dealer because you are so choosy when it comes to art and the art world.'

'Well then, let's see what you've got.'

Gideon turned on the spotlights and instructed the boys to begin. He had paced the showing of each canvas at four minutes apart. They were placed first on the easel and from there hung on the wall. Haver remained silent with not a change of expression throughout the display. His passive attitude unnerved Dendre. If he was an example of the art world, she knew she was in trouble.

Several times he did break his silence but only to ask, 'And when was that painted, Gideon?'

When all the paintings had been seen the boys rolled out a table stacked high with water-colours, pencil sketches and ink drawings which they held up for Haver to view. Finally it was over. The boys left the table and let themselves out of the studio

The first thing Haver did was to walk to Dendre, raise her hand and kiss it. Then he told her, 'Mrs Palenberg, you are not a wife, you are something more than that – Gideon's muse. My compliments.'

Gideon placed his arm around Dendre. 'That, coming from Haver, is praise indeed. His way of saying he's impressed. The question is, how much?'

'Enough to talk further with you about working together, and to ask you to put a reserve on five of the portraits I would like to buy outright. Enough to suggest you do not show these works to anyone else if you want us to do business together. What you have painted . . . well, Gideon, let's just say to have done what you have done in just a few years is a triumph.'

The two men threw their arms around each other and Haver said, 'This is a big night in the art world, only they don't know it yet.'

Both men laughed and walked together through the exhibition, talking about the paintings. It seemed to Dendre that the studio was suddenly charged with sizzling excitement, passion, what once were dreams bubbling into reality. Her head was spinning. All they had worked for, dreamed of, the hardships Gideon had suffered for his art – that book was closed. The two men were lost in the grip of dazzling creativity and were only wrenched back after more than two hours when Amber began to cry.

Dendre snapped out of her daze when she heard Gideon say, 'Come meet my daughter, Haver, she's lovely.'

After saying all the right things about Amber, Haver suggested, 'This night is cause for celebration. Come and dine with me. I'm having people in and it should be amusing but for the moment we'll say nothing about your work and my interest in representing you.'

'I understand. Anything you say, Haver. And we would love to come. If we can't find a sitter, it will have to be baby and all,' warned Gideon.

That evening in Haver's town house on 65th Street, Dendre saw the other side of the art world: beautiful, chic, intelligent women, with wealth beyond her imagining. Handsome and interesting men. Two famous artists whose smallest works sold for hundreds of thousands of dollars; their large commissions sold for millions. These were people who lived in houses with masterpieces hanging on the walls; who sat on eighteenth-century English, French or American furniture. At Haver's that evening they drank vintage champagne and ate fresh *fois gras*, caviar, stuffed pigeon breasts. Dendre was out of her depth; she worried about which fork to use, her hair, chapped hands, broken fingernails, Amber – who had been relegated to one of the five guest bedrooms, and most of all Gideon.

There were so many surprises for her that evening. They began the moment they were ushered into the house. The look on Haver's face when he greeted them suggested to Dendre that she did not look the part Haver would have liked her to play. She knew she looked too downmarket for her surroundings, too dull, and especially so walking into the drawing room flanked by Gideon's good looks and sensual charisma, and the urbane Haver. She wanted to die. Her confidence in herself plummeted.

Several people approached Gideon at once; the men shook hands, the women kissed him seductively on the lips. He seemed to rise to the occasion and Dendre knew she must somehow do the same. She was fidgeting and Gideon squeezed her hand and whispered as he kissed her on the cheek, 'Mustn't fidget, dear heart. You are better than all of them rolled into one. Play the art game, it's great fun.'

They had barely entered the room when that happened and she was surprised when Haver took her away. He marched her from the drawing room into his library. She stumbled and he caught her. She apologised, saying, 'Sorry, I couldn't take my eyes off the Soutine and wasn't looking where I was going. Are you going to represent Gideon, Mr Savage?'

Haver sat on the end of a huge, beautiful and impressive Louis XIV Boule desk. He reached for a cigarette and offered one to Dendre.

'I don't smoke, we can't afford to,' she told him rather petulantly.

Haver took his time lighting his cigarette, then told her, 'Well, that rather depends on terms. And on you.'

'Me!' she exclaimed.

'Yes, you. I want to be frank with you, Dendre. If Gideon and I do come to terms, I will not stand for any interference from you. It will have to be a one to one business relationship between Gideon and me. Now don't take this the wrong way. I will welcome you always as Gideon's wife, his muse, the woman behind the man, the model of his "Woman In Love" series, and respect you as such. I will be there to help you in that role in any way I can.

'But I have come across too many artists' wives who, when their husbands make it big, get greedy. They think they know better than his dealer how their husband should be handled. They see the prices their husbands' work commands, that art is first and foremost in his life and comes before wife and family. The dealer meanwhile is making huge profits, which I might tell you I hope to do representing Gideon, and so they undermine their husband's confidence in his business associate. Under the guise of protecting their husband's interests they go on the attack.

'Suddenly they want to step into the forefront of their husband's life and take over the running of his career. They want to come out of the shadows to present themselves as being more clever, more shrewd than the dealer who has spent years manipulating the art market to make certain their husbands are firmly entrenched in it. They see only how they have suffered neglect for art's sake. It is never enough for them to be wealthy beyond anything they have ever dreamed of, famous in the art world for being the wife of a genius. What they want to do, what they think is their right, is to run their husband's life, control his work, and turn themselves into art stars in their own right. I think that most succinctly states why we are having this talk and why whether I take Gideon on has everything to do with you.'

Dendre was astounded at the picture of the painter's wife he had drawn for her. Would she turn into one of those women Haver had described? It was too much even to contemplate. She collapsed into a chair, tears brimming in her eyes. She was out of her depth in this world of Haver Savage's, filled with successful, erudite men and stylish women, steeped in art and culture. She watched him rise from the desk and walk over to a drinks tray where he poured her a brandy. Walking back to the leather sofa where she was sitting, he handed it to her. She drank it down in one swallow and then coughed and spluttered.

In those few moments when she was trying to compose herself, Dendre made a firm decision: she wanted no part of the art world other than as Gideon's wife, the mainstay of his home and family, and most important of all his lover and muse. She vowed to herself that that was how it began and that was how it would end. That decision gave her a new kind of strength and power. It gave Dendre the courage to take on Haver.

'You have been candid with me, now I'll be candid with you. You have my word I will never interfere between my husband and any dealer he chooses to represent him. I have no interest in controlling his work nor do I want any power in the art world. As he himself has pointed out, I am Brooklyn born and bred. I like who I am and so does Gideon. That's why he loves me and married me. He is my life, his happiness is mine. Art is his world but it will only be a small part of mine – Gideon is far more important. Make no mistake, if fame and fortune do come our way he and I will reap the rewards but we will always remember to keep them in proportion to our life together.'

With every word she spoke Haver kept thinking how young she was, how naive, how obsessed with Gideon – and how little she really knew her husband. But he did believe her and had to accept that she was a strong and loyal young woman, one who would be the backbone of Gideon's life. He did not particularly like Dendre but did not feel strongly enough about her to dislike her either. She was an earth mother type, wearing long patterned skirts and glass beads. She had an interesting face devoid of cosmetics, a secret soul – not something he either admired or desired. He liked his women beautiful, intelligent, chic and decadent. He also knew that to be the kind of woman Gideon preferred for his notorious sexual escapades. No, Dendre would be no problem so long as she remained obsessively in love with her husband.

'That was quite a speech. I think you and I understand each other,' he said.

'Yes, I guess we do,' said Dendre with a smile, the tension she had been feeling thankfully dissolving.

'Even standing in Gideon's shadow, his fame and success may cause you problems. I want you to understand that you may call on me at any time, and if I can help I will.'

'That's very kind,' she answered, but the ice in her voice told Haver she would never call on him.

He couldn't help but think that she was wise to let him know they would never be friends, merely casual acquaintances. That suited him perfectly.

'Wait here a moment, will you, Dendre?'

Alone in the quiet of the library a terrible sadness came over her. She rose from the sofa where she had been sitting and walked to the open fire to lean on the mantelpiece. The honeymoon was over along with the hardships of the life she and Gideon had been living. He was getting everything he wanted and for that she was thankful. If she was certain of anything it was that whatever changes were happening in their life, the one thing Gideon would not want was for her to change. Rise to the occasion, yes, but not change herself or what they had together.

Haver returned to the room. Over his outstretched arms, he was carrying something wrapped in black tissue paper. He went directly to Dendre.

'This is for you. Would you do me the honour of accepting it?' he asked.

Dendre was nonplussed. She wanted no gift from Haver but instinct told her she was being ungracious. She felt decidedly awkward in this strange situation. Why had not Frieda taught her the proper way to handle such matters? Orlando came to mind. What would her brother do? He had a natural graciousness that she lacked. And then she worked it out by making herself believe she was Orlando.

'I would not be depriving the lady for whom you bought it?' she asked.

Rather a gracious way of accepting a gift, thought Haver. He was for the second time that night impressed with Dendre.

'It was for no specific lady. I buy beautiful things when I see them. I would really like you to have it and wear it this evening. I think it would suit you.'

With that she took the package from his arms and went to the desk where she carefully unwrapped a Chinese silk embroidered shawl. She was overcome by its beauty and hardly knew what to say so she said nothing, simply kept staring down at it. Haver finally picked it up and shook it out. The black silk shimmered in the light from the desk lamp. The plum-coloured embroidery was magnificent. Haver draped the shawl around her and tucked one end of it through the drab blue string belt she was wearing over an ill-fitting, worn black knit dress.

'It suits you just fine, Dendre,' he told her.

He fluffed her hair and pinched her cheeks to colour them then stood back and looked at her. 'You're a handsome woman, Dendre.'

'Now that you've fixed me up,' she said knowingly and with some petulance in her voice. His condescension was irritating to her. His world was a foreign place and not one she really cared to visit.

She only now began to understand what Gideon had meant when in those first days after they had married he had told her, 'You know, Dendre, the reason this marriage is working so well is not only because we love each other but because we are so different and respect those differences. We dip our toes into each other's lives and gain something special from the experience.'

It came as a shock to her to see that Gideon was right. They would each of them lead separate lives because she was no more suited to live his than he was hers. Tonight she was dipping her toes into Gideon's world and she was going to make certain she damn' well made a good job of it, enjoyed what she could of it, and kept her own counsel. She was about to make her debut as Gideon's adoring wife, his faithful shadow, stylishly adorned by Haver so as not to show him up.

Dendre and Gideon may have bussed it up to Haver Savage's town house but they returned home in Haver's chauffeur-driven Rolls-Royce. Dendre was waiting for Gideon to say something about the evening but he remained silent. Sitting in the back seat with Amber in her Moses basket between them, Dendre kept running the events of the night through her mind. Gideon had been so at ease, so charming, he'd gathered the guests around him without even trying. They'd adored him. He was amusing, utterly disarming, so much more powerful than anyone else in the room. Every time she found herself alone or out of her depth in conversation with someone, he would be there to save her or include her in the group he was with. She could see envy in the other women, wondering as to how she could have captured his heart.

Gideon leaned over the Moses basket and kissed Dendre on the cheek. He took her hand in his but said nothing. It was she who finally broke the silence. 'You seemed right at home with those people. Happy even.'

'I was and I am. Not at all your scene, I know. But never mind, you'll get used to the art world and make your own place in it,' he told her, and that was the end of it. He turned away from her and looked through the automobile window, watching New York City at night flash by.

Chapter 8

Gideon was a joy to sleep with. Going to bed with him was always an adventure, and not just a sexual one. This was the time when he chose to discuss his work with Dendre or to speak about their life together – how much he loved her and Amber. He also talked about his dreams and aspirations. And this was the time he listened to her opinions and considered them. Dendre soon realised that six in the morning was truly their most intimate hour of the day when he belonged only to her. After that Gideon thought only of his painting and his freedom.

Since he had known her, there had never been a night when, last thing before falling asleep, he did not hold her in his arms and kiss her, not a morning when he didn't awaken her with a kiss. More often than not, that first kiss fired him sexually and they would start the day only after they had sated their lust in orgasm.

Arriving home from Haver's, both she and Gideon were for too charged up to sleep. Gideon was especially effervescent, bubbling over with happiness. He was high as a kite that had broken away and was rising higher and higher on a soft, warm wind. Dendre saw an aura of wild passion around him. She wanted to be where he was and was drawn to it, actually gave herself over to it. After settling Amber she went to the middle of the studio where she found her husband sitting on the chair Haver had last sat in, contemplating his own work. His eyes were bright with excitement. She imagined how fast his heart must be beating, pounding even. She knew her own was.

Gideon turned away from the paintings at the first sound of her footsteps. He held out his hand to Dendre and she took it and was guided by him to stand before him. He had a strange and exciting glint in his eyes that she could not remember seeing before. It was terrifyingly sexy, depraved even. All she could think was how much she wanted to be perverted from her virtue and morality. To be more intemperate and sensual than any other woman had ever been. She saw in his eyes a man who could and had been a viciously sensual man, one who enjoyed sex in that way. Until now, in their erotic life together, he had only hinted that he could be such a man. Dendre had never taken those suggestions seriously until this moment. Now she wanted to be his debauchee, to reap the sexual thrills of anything that might give them both the ultimate orgasm. She felt as if she had been holding back on the wilder shores of sex and therefore cheating them both.

Standing in front of Gideon, she asked him in a voice husky with lust as she undid the belt round her waist and handed it to him, 'Are you going to take Haver Savage as your dealer?'

He watched his wife seductively slide the shawl from her shoulders and let it slip to the floor. She could feel the sexual excitement coming off him as she raised her dress over her head and provocatively threw it in his lap. She stood before him naked save for her white stockings held up by garters of lace around the top of her thighs. Days after they began living together he had decided she would always remain naked under her outer garments, open and ready for sex wherever and whenever either one of them wished to give vent to their lust.

Gideon could hardly take his eyes off her body, sexual heat shimmering in his eyes. She cupped her breasts in her hands, pinched her nipples. She struck erotic poses and her naked body shone in the light, incredibly voluptuous. He was brimming with delight, thinking of the many ways he would fuck her tonight. He was thrilled with this sexual protégée of his. He had taught her to love sex and orgasm, her own body, a man's penis, and she revelled in his teachings. She was now a woman experienced in erotic hunger and how to sate that particular appetite. He loved her for her submissiveness, her obsession with him, her strength and willingness to pay any price so as to remain by his side as wife, lover, friend.

She was constantly surprising Gideon by her steely determination to rise above her own limitations so that she might add to his life. In private she was changing while in public she remained the passably pretty, rather limited wife of Gideon Palenberg. Perversely, he liked her limitations, her dullness, as much as he enjoyed the other Dendre behind firmly locked doors. It suited him, he actually loved her more for it. They both appreciated that she saved him from having to take care of himself. That was the power she wielded over him.

Gideon rose from his chair and went to her. 'Yes, if Haver and I can strike a deal that suits us both, I will go with him.' While he spoke he tied her belt tightly around her breasts, making them appear even more voluptuous than they already were. They were firm, the skin taut, round, and her nipples oozing mother's milk. She looked terrifyingly sexy, incredibly raunchy, spurting milk, her stance defiant, challenging.

'Do you like Haver?' he asked as he fondled her breasts.

'No,' she answered. Her voice had a tremor in it.

Gideon knew that tremor well. When out of control with sexual desire, it was always there in her voice. She was being particularly assertive with her sexuality tonight and he admired that in women just as much as when they suddenly collapsed in total submission to a man's sexual demands.

'You will get used to him. After me he is going to be the most important man in your life,' he told her.

'Let's just forget him for now,' she pleaded.

'Forgotten,' Gideon told her, and lowered his head to take one of her nipples in his mouth and suck hard from her breast.

Dendre thought she might swoon, so powerfully sexy was it to have her husband suckling from her breast. She felt both ecstasy and pain: Gideon feeding from her nipple, the tight belt tied around her breasts. The sensations were exquisite. She groaned, she whined, she came. She begged him to stop.

'Oh, no. This is just the beginning,' he told her, then bent to her other breast.

His searching fingers found her wet and warm with overflowing lust. He used them to bring her on and between the force of his penetration and his mouth sucking her dry of milk she went quite over the edge of sex into a yearning for any sort of depraved sensation she had not previously tasted nor imagined. She told that to Gideon who was in much the same state.

He all but tore his clothes from his body and told her while doing so: 'You are sublime like this, thrilling. You excite me beyond measure with your lust for me.'

He untied her breasts and now draped the belt around her neck, leading her to a pipe that ran down the wall. He bound her wrists together first then turned her to the wall and tied her to the pipe. He left her for a few minutes, returning with a scarf that he put round her eyes.

Fear had gripped her, yet she was also feeling a new kind of excitement. 'I don't think I like this,' she told him.

But Gideon was not there. He had gone to the fridge to fetch one of the bottles of champagne Haver had sent home with them. She called to him several times and still there was no answer. It was quiet in the studio, even the silence felt sexy. She was cold and her heart was racing. Then she heard a shot and jumped.

'What was that?' she asked.

And this time Gideon did answer. 'This is a game of trust, depraved sex, and love. Did you think I was shooting at you?'

'No. I know you'll never harm me.'

'Right answer. Now you get a glass of champagne,' he told her.

He went to her and after ordering her to open her mouth, poured the wine into it slowly so she would not gag. It dribbled from her mouth and ran down her body. Gideon licked the rivulets on to his tongue. He took several swigs of the wine before he placed the bottle on the floor and untied Dendre from the pipe. With the belt still round her neck, he led her to a blanket he had spread on the floor.

She found it oddly thrilling to have sex with a man she could not see. Once lust had overtaken her and reason was abandoned, Gideon ceased to exist for her. There was only his mouth, his lips, his rampant penis, his caressing hands and sometimes vicious thrusting, the sting of her belt on her flesh when she broke the silence he insisted upon. She lost count of her many orgasms, of the times he had come. She could only remember how divine it was still to have the taste of him in her mouth, to submit to his every sexual demand.

They continued their sexual extravaganza for hours and she dozed in his arms from time to time. When Gideon finally took her blindfold off and untied her hands she saw for the first time the bruising round her breasts where he had first tied the belt, and also that he had turned her into a living Palenberg painting while she had been asleep. The nimbuses around her nipples were painted a light amber colour; the nipples red and bruised from his sucking, had been left as they were. There was a chain painted round her neck in dark blue; lovely designs in a henna colour on her arms and legs.

'I'm more beautiful than I ever imagined I could be,' she told him with tears of pleasure in her eyes.

Spent himself, he wanted still to see her come once more as his creation. He used an object of jade, Japanese, seventeenth-century, carved into a handsome sculpted penis. It had been a gift from Haver during the time when he'd first arrived in New York and they had spent days and nights enjoying sexual orgies with several luscious ladies.

He found it extraordinarily erotic to control Dendre by sex and orgasm. Even more so tonight when the world was his and he had painted her, marked her as his creation, a work of art that only they in their lust would see. Her orgasm was strong and copious. When, for the last time, he removed the jade from her cunt it glistened as if dipped in nectar and he licked it clean.

He raised her from the floor and took her to the bath where he washed her. She was too exhausted to speak, her heart full of love and passion from having seen him lick her come. How many men loved a woman enough to enjoy her like that? Not many, she was certain. And once more she was grateful for his love and lust for her.

Lying next to her in bed, he kissed her good night and told her what a marvellous lover she was. He promised her similar nights of splendour would be theirs forever.

Later he kissed Dendre awake and placed a docile Amber next to her.

'It's very late. I've seen to her already so you might have an easy morning.'

'Where are you going?' asked Dendre.

'I have an eleven o'clock meeting with Haver.'

Dendre sprang to life and sat up in bed. She had never slept so deeply nor awakened so late in the day. Her morning kiss had in the past come no later then six o'clock. Gideon liked to be at his easel no later than seven, no matter how late in the evening he might have been working. She felt somehow disorientated: her husband was dressed for uptown in his black coat with its velvet collar. He was not lying next to her to press that morning kiss upon her, but instead had given her Amber as a replacement.

She kissed her baby and wondered if Gideon was already drifting away from her. Husband and wife gazed into each other's eyes and she waited for some small sign of reassurance that this was not the case. She very nearly shouted with joy when she received what she most desperately needed: a second kiss for her and one on Amber's forehead.

'I'll be home as soon as I can. But that may not be until early evening, possibly even later. I intend to hammer out all the details of the deal with Haver so we never have to do it again.'

When Gideon returned home triumphant it was nearly eleven in the evening. Dendre had placed the small table they dined at close to the fireplace. The moment she heard the intercom buzzer go with his signal, she lit the candles and fussed with the small arrangement of flowers she had splurged on with what little money that was left in their weekly budget. Her afternoon had been spent cooking a celebratory meal for them on the two-ring electric cooker:

chicken in a cream-and-mushroom sauce with buttered rice, ice cream with her home-made butterscotch sauce and walnuts. His favourite meal. The second bottle of champagne that Haver had given them the night before stood cooling in the galvanised bucket she used to mop the floor.

Gideon was moved by the sight of the small table and lit candles, Dendre standing by the open fire, Amber in her arms. His wife and his child, the goodness and purity of their souls, stood out as bright stars against the drab and harsh surroundings of the loft.

He went to Dendre and kissed her and the baby. 'You may not like change, dear Dendre, but you certainly rise to it. How did you know I hadn't dined out?'

'I didn't. But this is home and we always eat at home except when we go out with my mother and father,' she told him.

'I made my deal with Haver, got everything I wanted and so did he. I feel like the happiest man on earth. Also the hungriest.'

She pulled the bucket up off the floor and handed it to Gideon and they both laughed. Her toast to him was: 'Watch out, world. The Palenbergs have arrived!'

In those first years after Haver took Gideon on, the three Palenbergs remained in the studio, living very much as they always had except for a larger budget. But there were drastic changes in their social life. They now had one. They went out more, mostly to first nights of exhibitions. They entertained art pundits and painters, even a few collectors. A visit to Gideon Palenberg's studio became a much sought after invitation. Gideon could now afford to drink and did, only the best champagne.

But Gideon and Dendre had been too poor and too hungry,

had worked too hard, to be frivolous with the advance of money Haver gave them every month. Half went into the bank and they lived on the remainder. Dendre kept their accounts in order.

Once word was out that Haver Savage had a new discovery the art world flocked to The Haver Savage Gallery, but in vain. There were only two paintings to be seen and neither was for sale. It was eleven months before the doors opened on the first one-man show of Gideon's work. Everyone who was anyone in the New York art world was there.

But of those present no one was more excited and less surprised by the astonishing brilliance of the exhibition than Herschel, Frieda, and Orlando.

Gideon saw them enter the gallery. He had imagined they might feel out of their depth, looking their old, middle-class, styleless selves, feeling uncomfortable among the sophisticated and elegantly turned out crowd. Not in the least. Orlando had obviously taken Herschel in hand and delivered him to Brooks Brothers. He looked more like an Ivy League professor than a furrier. Harvard had taught Orlando that it was more than a university. It was a way of life. He was as well dressed as his father.

But Frieda! She was standing at the entrance to the room, head held high, and wearing her pride on the sleeve of her black mink, brilliantly tailored, short jacket. Her skirt of black suede had been the perfect choice to complete her ensemble. Gideon wove his way through the viewers directly to them. When he shook Herschel's hand, Gideon thought his father-in-law would burst into tears of joy.

'You look like a Harvard professor, Herschel,' said Gideon.

'And you,' said Herschel, 'look like you always look, a huge success.' Then the two men hugged each other.

When they parted, Gideon raised Frieda's hand and lowered his head to kiss it. 'Frieda, you look amazingly elegant and sophisticated,' he told her as he touched the small, pill box, suede hat sitting on top of her head.

'Sophisticated? Elegant? What are you talking about, Gideon? The jacket belongs to my sister, Rose, the hat belongs to Leona Shwartz, and the skirt is a French label I can't pronounce but neither could the sales girl at Lohman's basement sale. But chic it is, I have been assured, and all because we don't want to let the side down. I'm very proud and bursting with happiness for you, Gideon, and, of course, for my Dendre. A dream come true for you both.'

Gideon kissed his mother-in-law on both cheeks. Dendre joined them just as Gideon moved to kiss Orlando and they shook hands firmly, reflecting their deep friendship and affection for one another.

He should have known Dendre's family would rise to the occasion.

On the first night sixty per cent of the paintings were sold. Thirty-five per cent more went in the first week. It was an unequivocal triumph. The London exhibition was not such a success until a month later when the art news magazines and the newspaper critics had covered it in England. Seventy-five per cent of the drawings and water-colours were then sold.

Mercifully the Palenbergs still had no telephone in the studio. If there had been it would never have stopped ringing with strangers offering invitations or seeking them. Instead Gideon's post and telephone messages went to the gallery and thence to the studio, delivered by one of Haver's minions. She was usually a pretty, chic, bright, young woman who would willingly respond to Gideon's seductive charm.

The first time Dendre noticed how much attention he was showing the girl, even to walking her from the studio to the street with his arm around her, she blanked it from her mind. After the third and fourth time Dendre felt hurt but reassured herself that her husband loved her, and so what if he was a flirt? How had she not known that he liked to charm ladies? she asked herself, and realised that she and Gideon had happened too fast. He had swept her off her feet before she had even got to know him. They had married with him remaining secretive about himself and his life before Dendre. She was appalled that she really did not know her husband, the father of her child, the man she loved beyond life itself. It was too late to question him now. They had lived a day-to-day existence and a happy life together. Dendre made one of her vows. As long as she was loved by Gideon and they had a life together, she would never question, just wait for him to reveal himself to her.

At dinner one evening he announced, 'We're going out tonight, to a Greek place I know. It has the best *bouzouki* you will find outside of Greece.'

'It's eleven o'clock, Gideon, and we have no sitter nor will I find one at this hour.'

'I bumped into Valdez and asked him to come to sit with Amber. He should be here any minute.'

Valdez was one of the two boys he had picked up in the street to help when he was showing work to the dealers. Valdez was a street-wise boy who turned out to be very quick to learn. As soon as the advance of money arrived he was worked into the Palenberg budget. He adored Amber and often took care of her.

Gideon had hardly finished his sentence when the intercom went and Gideon buzzed the boy in. He assured Dendre, 'You will love the place and the man who runs it. Just average food, but great belly dancers and sailors off Greek cargo ships who dance their hearts and souls out on the tiny dance floor. Lots of smashing of plates – a million light years away from the art world game. Gregarious and hospitable people, the Greeks. The first thing we'll do when we have real money is buy a house on the Island of Hydra and spend half the year there. It's a marvellous place, I lived there for a couple of years once.'

The Greek restaurant-cum-night club was in an even more seedy street than the one where they lived. They could hear the music halfway up the street. A great fuss was made of Gideon there. They had a marvellous time and, now that they could afford it, it became their favourite place for a night out.

In the weeks that followed, Dendre found her niche in this new life she and Gideon had worked so hard to secure. Her husband's comfort, his every sexual desire, the kitchen, Amber and the new baby she was carrying became her life. She was determined to do right by her extraordinary man. She studied gourmet French cooking, Italian, Japanese and Chinese too. She excelled in flower arranging and studied Greek, a must if they were eventually to live in Greece. She walked Fifth and Madison Avenues pushing her pram and window shopped, gathering ideas, learning, learning, learning.

Haver became important in their lives because they could appreciate the professionalism of the way he represented Gideon. There was no question that Haver and Gideon had a rapport between them, trusted in each other's ability. Dendre took Haver's advice and never interfered. It was enough for her that Gideon continued to discuss his work with her, seek her opinion, and as often as not act upon it. The money kept accumulating in their bank account as for five years they lived a frugal life. It was a joint decision between Dendre and Gideon, who both wished never again to live on handouts. When Daisy was born, it was impossible for them to remain living in the studio. They took on an apartment that was hardly better than their former living quarters because it was within walking distance of the studio. It did at least have central heating, hot and cold running water, a proper four-burner cooker with an oven.

This was a successful rather than a happy time for Dendre and Gideon because circumstances were separating them. Success, respect for his work, took all the pressures of the mundane out of Gideon's life. Haver was running his art life and Dendre his home life and he was left to paint. Haver, as well as his artist friends, could not believe his meanness, keeping his old rundown studio and Dendre and his children in an apartment only the most desperate would have rented. She still worked at home as a bookkeeper for her original clients. Gideon replied to their criticism by saying, 'Because I have a little money, do I necessarily have to change my lifestyle? I've always been kept by women, my Aunt Martha then Dendre. It suits me just fine.'

He truly loved his wife and children but loved painting even more. The years rolled by and he was proved to be consistently brilliant. The international art world, museums, the best collectors, bought his paintings. He was now an art star and enjoying his success in that world. His paintings were selling on average for $650,000 a canvas. The day that a Gideon Palenberg portrait of Dendre was sold to the Museum of Modern Art in New York for in excess of $1,000,000, he took his wife to lunch at the Café Cholson. It was dimly lit by artful pinpoint lights and candles, and decorated with baskets of fresh fruits and vegetables spilling over from stunning marble pedestal bowls and plates. Whole cured hams rested on silver platters beside pyramids of crushed ice studded with oysters. All glistened under the lights beaming down on the massive marble console.

Dendre was dazzled by such chic: the navy blue walls, the deep-plum-coloured velvet banquettes, the huge palm trees. 'Oh, Gideon, I love it here. What fun – and how romantic, dining by candlelight in the middle of the day.'

She kissed him on the cheek, stunned for a moment by that charisma of his that was even more powerful and seductive today. Sexuality seemed to ooze from every pore of his body. How had she not noticed he was impossibly attractive and wearing his success like a royal robe? His eyes were roaming the room and settled from time to time on a pretty young face. She saw several women looking at him. Silently she was telling them, Back off, he's mine. That was the moment she realised that Gideon had other women.

He told her, 'I knew you would like it here,' a smile of delight on his face that she did.

Did he compare her with the others? Did having them make him love her more? Dendre blanked off the realisation that her husband was being unfaithful. It was easy when she rationalised that he did at least love her and the children; that he still found her sexually attractive, in fact more so than ever. That was evident in his strong libido and the adventurous sex life they had together.

By the time they were seated the very idea that Gideon would betray her had vanished from her mind. He ordered a bottle of champagne. The waiter seemed to know him, which surprised Dendre. She would have been happier had they discovered the place together. A dealer, Ben Borgnine and Dominique Andros, a famous painter, were just leaving the restaurant together and stopped to greet Dendre and Gideon. She liked them both. It was easy to like Ben Borgnine who always made a point of spending time with her during

116

important exhibitions or parties when everyone else was busily working the floor to meet as many art celebrities as possible. Everyone but Dendre was afraid of the volatile Dominique but admired her work and her dedication to art. She adored Gideon, had always championed his work, had opened to him all the important doors in fine art society that counted when he had first arrived in New York. That life of hustling for attention that he had given up only a few weeks before he met his wife was not something Dendre could easily equate with her proud, independent husband.

The daughter of a famous French writer and a Greek poet, Dominique had *entrée* to the best houses round the world. A passionate artist obsessed with her work and the art world, she used everyone who crossed her path to further herself and the many artists she championed. She was a secretive creature who knew the rich and famous of the art world in both Europe and the States well enough to call them friends.

This Athenian-born lady, respected for her work and adored by the international art world even though she was volatile, difficult, and notorious for having both men and women as lovers, was in love with Dendre. Several times she had made overtures to her, seeking to get her into bed. Dendre had never understood how badly Dominique wanted her sexually. It had been Gideon who had explained it to her. Not so much shocked as sad for the other woman, Dendre had worked hard at being a good friend to her but the two of them never discussed the issue.

Ben and Dominique left them to study the menu. Looking over the top of his, Gideon said, 'Is it a turn on to have both Ben and Dominique yearning to have sex with you?'

'Ben?' exclaimed Dendre.

'You must pay more attention to detail. Those little nuances that are hints.'

'Not possible! That's your imagination on overdrive,' she said laughingly.

'Maybe so,' he conceded.

But now that it been said, it stuck in her mind. She did like the idea that Ben was sexually attracted to her. It was an ego boost and for the first time she wondered what it would be like to have sex with a man other than Gideon. She laughed aloud, wondering what it would be like to have sex with both Gideon and Ben at the same time.

'How wicked you can be, Gideon,' she reproved her husband.

'Why wicked, my love?'

'Planting that seed in my head when you know you are enough for me in the erotic compartment of my life. Wicked because I know you. You are planning something to which you want me to acquiesce. Something depraved and delicious,' she whispered.

There was a sexy aura around them now. Gideon reached across the table and took Dendre's hand. He rose from his chair, leaned over the table and kissed it. She was consumed with love for him.

Chapter 9

'I have some news, and it's only right for you to be the first one to hear it,' said Gideon in between the oysters and the fillet of beef with *Sauce Béarnaise*.

'It must be good news or we wouldn't be lunching. Do tell?'

'It's happened, my success is assured. Haver sold a painting of mine to a museum in Dallas for one million, three hundred thousand dollars. Dendre, my paintings have made us very wealthy and always will. Everything I told you when we first met has come true.'

Dendre, who was after all their bookkeeper, knew already they were wealthy beyond anything she had ever hoped for. 'I'm so happy for you, Gideon. For us,' she said.

'Now we can enjoy the luxuries of life. We'll buy a house in Greece – no, two, close to each other, and make one into a studio. And two lofts, one above the other, here in the city. One to work in and one for our family. Would you like that?'

'It sounds so grand. Of course I would like to live like that!'

'Now we can afford the luxury of the sun and the sea, occasional travel to far off places. But most important of all I can retreat from the social aspect of painting, become a recluse, just work and enjoy my girls.'

Dendre caught his excitement. She visualised the life he described and her own enjoyment bubbled over into gay abandon. Gideon sat back in his chair and watched his wife who seemed to bloom before his eyes.

He thought of something else then and immediately sobered. 'Aunt Martha – I would like you to calculate how much money she has sent me since you came into my life, double the amount and write out a cheque.'

'That's very generous of you considering you're so bitter about her. I'll take care of it tomorrow.'

'Maybe if I pay her off, I'll be rid of her for good. I did so hate taking her money. But it meant survival, and without it who knows where I would be now?'

'I don't think you dislike her as much as you claim to. And why do you anyway?'

'Then you'd be wrong. My mother was Aunt Martha's only sister. My father the poor relation of a socially prominent, well-to-do family who settled in St Louis from Copenhagen in the late seventeen-hundreds. He was madly in love with my mother but they had a star-crossed marriage. When I was five years old my mother developed cancer. She suffered great pain that neither she nor my father could bear. One day they dropped me off at Aunt Martha's and went home. When they were found later that day by my aunt, who was having a tea party that afternoon and had no time for a mischievous boy, they were lying side by side in their bed. My father had shot my mother and then himself.

'He was a meticulous man. He left a note for the police, one for his attorney, one for Aunt Martha and one for me. I was eight years old.

'It was a huge scandal which my aunt deeply resented. She had little choice but to take me in as my father had requested. She was part of St Louis high society with more class than cash, just as my father and mother were. Not to take me in would have been impossible if she wanted to keep her good name.'

It was obvious by the expression on Dendre's face that she was horrified by her husband's story. It explained so much about Gideon's behaviour; why he loved her, her parents, Orlando, all of whom were steeped in family affection.

Gideon drained his glass and refilled it. He took one more sip and said, 'I have never discussed my early life with anyone before. Best you hear the rest so we never have to speak of it again.

'Aunt Martha, who had never liked me or my father, thought that my mother could have done much better. She had been a great beauty and the family was one of the best in St Louis. I don't think my aunt ever forgave her. She gave me a room in the servants' quarters when there were seven master bedrooms. She was demanding and parsimonious. It was a loveless upbringing filled with petty humiliations, even poverty, in a grand turn-of-the-century house. I saw her rarely and ate my meagre meals with the servants. I was always hungry. After school it was chores. When I was eighteen she gave me the money my father had left me, three thousand dollars, and a stipend from her so long as I didn't return to St Louis.

'She said on my departure, "You are a stubborn boy, but talented. Go make yourself into something. We'll exchange Christmas cards." We never did. She never missed sending the monthly cheque but never a word of greeting or kindness with it.'

Dendre felt his pain as he was telling her this dreadful story. When he stopped talking they remained silent for several seconds. The silence was broken by the waiter bringing them their main course. After the young man had gone from the table, Dendre said, 'I'll send the money first thing in the morning.' And made no other comment.

Gideon thought to himself, How fine of her not to ask questions. Any other woman would have. He felt a rush of happiness coursing through his veins. He had always considered Aunt Martha's hand outs as cold charity. Somehow being able to return her money set him free from her hatred. It no longer seemed to matter than she had been so cold, so unloving. That was over, the past was the past.

'Dendre, I have a surprise for you,' he said. 'You know how much Frieda and Herschel want to move to Florida for the winters. Well, I want to give them an apartment there. Orlando is in Miami now, looking for one. There was a message from him at the gallery saying he has found one on the beach he is certain they would be thrilled with. There are even several people from Brooklyn in the apartment building. I called Orlando back and bought it for them. He's coming here to New York in time for the family outing on Sunday and I will give them the deeds to the place then.'

Dendre was nonplussed, overwhelmed by his generosity. Comparatively recently they had been watching every dollar. Her father was still picking up the bill for their Sunday outings. Her parents had not the vaguest idea how wealthy Gideon and she now were. To Dendre the money in the bank account was just abstract figures that kept adding up. Hardly reality because they had never drawn any out for extravagances. Now, suddenly, those figures were houses and apartments and old debts repaid. She couldn't possibly know how to deal with spending so much. But Gideon did and would teach her.

'That is so generous. They yearned to make a move to Florida but it was just a daydream, unattainable. And you've made it come true.'

Dendre rose from her chair and went to kiss Gideon. They smiled at each other and she went back to her seat to finish her meal.

It was only later, going home on the bus, that she realised what was happening to them. Gideon was sweeping away the past, making way for a new life. Once more she would have to meet the challenge. Once more she would have to make an effort to fit in with Gideon's celebrity. She had no worries about that; she had become strong and sure of herself as Gideon Palenberg's wife. These new changes would be but a further refinement of that, she told herself.

It was a matter of days after that lunch at the Café Cholson that Dendre realised how easily Gideon was slipping into the role of great painter, another Picasso, Miro, Rothko. The world was at his feet and he was spinning it any way he wanted to while she lagged faithfully behind, his shadow, his keeper.

The next few years brought another child into their lives, and three new residences: on the Island of Hydra in Greece, on Fire Island, and a vast duplex studio-cum-home in the city. It brought too, for the first time, separations. Gideon would on occasion make a trip: to be present for the hanging of a show, to talk to architects and builders working on one of their houses or his studios. Dendre would be left behind though he would call at least once a day. The children and running three houses gave her a life as busy as her husband's. Being wife of Gideon Palenberg, mother of his three daughters, was a full-time job.

They lived a grand and exciting life now. When the children were old enough they were sent to the best private school in New York City. That was why Gideon acquired the Fire Island property: easy access from New York by water taxi, then quiet and seclusion so he could work undisturbed. No more was their life the simple togetherness of two people in love. There were now assistants for Gideon; maids, cleaners and house boys for Dendre to ease her load.

One afternoon, while she was window shopping on Madison, she stopped to look at a massive marble vase filled with an assortment of white lilies. They were breathtakingly beautiful. Ever since Haver took Gideon on, fresh flowers had been included in the household budget. She was wondering whether to buy them or not when she looked through the window into the shop. Gideon was buying flowers – the lilies in the window. The assistant walked away from him and began taking the flowers from the vase, stem by stem. She looked up once and smiled at Dendre who very nearly went in to join her husband but thought she might be ruining his surprise so instead scuttled away from the shop.

He arrived home late that evening empty-handed. The flowers had not been delivered. She had a difficult time keeping calm, asking no questions. Instinct told her that it would be the wrong thing to do. The right thing would be to face the obvious: he had another woman. She rose above that torture and put it firmly to the back of her mind.

The children were asleep and so there were only the two of them dining together. Gideon was flattering about the meal, seemed happy and vital. After dinner they went down to his studio and talked about the house being renovated on Fire Island while he worked. It was midnight when the intercom buzzed. Dendre jumped at the sound. Gideon placed his brushes in a jug and turned the easel to the wall. The intercom went again.

He went to Dendre and kissed her then told her, 'It's only Terry.'

She felt relieved that it was someone she liked and told him,

'He'll be hungry, looking for a meal. I'll go upstairs and put something together for him.'

'I'll open a bottle of wine,' Gideon told her.

Terry was about the same age as Dendre, a sculptor whom Gideon thought showed real promise. He and Dendre had befriended the young man who often dropped in on them. He was rather a wild and free soul who had many times told Dendre and Gideon of the orgies he'd enjoyed attending. Dendre had often been titillated by tales of his sex life.

Terry ate his food with gusto and they all drank far too much. By now they were sitting on the double bed covered with a wolf skin blanket that Gideon kept in his studio so he might stretch out on it when he needed a break from work. It was where he and Dendre had their more erotic and adventurous sex.

Dendre realised that Terry was high on more than wine. He seemed to her to be speeding, even more outrageous than usual. Gideon was enchanted with him, found Terry stimulating, a fresh new thinker. It was two in the morning when their guest began caressing Dendre. Embarrassed, she moved away from him. He slid closer to her and kissed her on the cheek, her neck, the lobes of her ears. She was aroused by his advances but broke the spell by standing up.

'Gideon, your wife is the sexiest woman . . . but then, you must already know that. Let's undress and go to bed, the three of us.'

'I've never seen my wife having sex with two men. How would you like that, dear heart? I would like it enormously.'

Dendre was shocked. Gideon approved of her having another man. He actually wanted a threesome. She had had too much to drink and her resistance was low, her libido stronger than her morals. She considered it and sat down again between her husband and Terry. Gideon kissed her passionately and she yielded to him. He undid the buttons on her blouse and kissed her again as he slipped it off her shoulder. Terry saw Dendre transform herself from the placid, rather boring woman he and the world knew into a seductive lady with lust in her eyes, a hunger to be riven and sated.

He caressed her breasts before settling his mouth over the nipple of one. Dendre reluctantly pushed him away. Gideon took Terry's place at the same breast. She found it exciting, and a little frightening. The two men continued caressing her. She came and called out, unable to keep her immense pleasure to herself.

To Dendre the very air the three of them were breathing seemed to be erotically charged. Yet she forced herself to grab for her blouse. Things were going too far. Terry was too quick for her. He flung it away and took her hands, kissing them.

'For a long time I've wanted to have sex with you and Gideon,' he said. 'I dream of Gideon and me both fucking you at the same time. Doesn't that excite you? Don't pretend it doesn't. Let yourself go sexually – you'll love it.'

She very nearly laughed. He had no suspicion that she always let herself go when it came to sex with Gideon; that she was far more depraved with her husband than any women Terry had ever had.

She looked at Gideon and said, 'I don't want to do this.'

'I would like you to. It would be thrilling for you and excite me to share you with Terry,' he told her.

'I would never want to share you with another woman.'

'But you will if I ask you to,' he said.

'I'm afraid. You are the only man I've ever been with, and what if people find out?'

'I promise I will never tell a soul,' said Terry. 'And if I did, they wouldn't believe it of you.'

There was more pleading from Dendre but neither Gideon

nor Terry let up on her. It was dawn when Terry finally let himself out of the studio. Dendre slept on until midday. Gideon woke her with her usual morning kiss and told her how much he loved her, that she was the most sensual woman he had ever had, and kissed her and fondled her breasts.

Why had he picked that night to have a threesome? He was a cheat and had other women, and now she had been had by another man. What was he telling her? That it was all right for her to take a lover? That it piqued his lust, his love of adventurous sex? Gideon had yet again seduced her, charmed her into a sexual adventure. She had done it to please him and as a result had had an extraordinary night of sexual bliss. Whenever she acquiesced to his wishes she always benefited.

'Gideon, I went shopping yesterday and passed a florist's,' she told him. 'They had only one thing displayed in the window: lilies. Long-stemmed, large-headed white lilies, Arum, Longe and Casablanca. I contemplated buying them all for us, they were so marvellous.'

'What stopped you, Dendre?' he asked brazenly.

'I saw you writing a card to go with them.'

'You're not going to ask who I sent them to?'

'No. I just want you to know that no matter how discreet you are, it still hurts. Although a little less each time.'

'Good, my love,' he told her, and took her in his arms.

Dendre said no more. There was little she could say. It was one of those situations where one more word might tip the balance and their life together would be damaged or, worse still, over.

'Dendre, I never want you to be hurt by my flirtations. Just remember, they are a passing fancy. Of no more importance than that in our lives. I will always love you more than any of them,' he told her as he caressed her and they gazed into each other's eyes.

Dendre could see that it was true. It was what she needed to hear to close her mind to his other women. She had the ability immediately to block out anything unpleasant, pretend it had never happened. She put that to work now and asked Gideon if he would like pancakes for breakfast.

From that day on Dendre pulled back considerably from the social side of the art world and gave her husband what he had always wanted from her; a family life to come home to. She deduced that the less she saw of his flirtations, the easier it would be on her. The one thing she knew for sure was that he loved her, needed her as much as she needed him. She had a place in his life that no dalliance could undermine. Where would he find a wife as tolerant of everything he wanted and blessed with enough strength and love to give it to him? He had laid down the ground rules before they were married; he meant to be a free man with a life of his own and to have one with her on his terms. Now, all these years later, he was still that man and she as his wife would give him what he wanted. Still very much in love with Gideon and living an exciting life, she retreated more into the background. Her happiest times were when they stayed on Fire Island or in the Hydra house where he worked feverishly, assisted by his now well-trained helpers. Those times she had him all to herself.

As time went by, without even realising it, Dendre created a life of her own: being the wife of Gideon Palenberg, bringing up her daughters, dealing with the now large staff who followed them everywhere. Most important of all, being sexually active and loved.

At a first night exhibition and dinner at the Museum of Modern Art which she attended with Gideon, she hardly had a chance to walk with him through the gallery. He was swept away by dozens of people who wanted to speak with the now great man of art. At dinner he flirted outrageously with a beautiful young woman. For one moment Dendre found it intolerable, then her anxiety faded when she reminded herself he was free to do as he wanted. She had agreed that before they were married.

Ben Borgnine was sitting to her left and Max Ernst to her right. Ben had always been interested in her; Max thought her boring and insignificant. She turned to Ben who was talking to the girl on his left.

'Ben, remember me, I'm still here,' she whispered in his ear.

He laughed and after a few more words with the other lady, turned to look at Dendre. 'I may have been making chit-chat but you know you are always in my thoughts.'

'I think I like that,' she told him, and realised it was actually true. 'Why?' she asked happily.

'Because you and I have a great deal in common. We are both obsessed with Gideon. Me with his paintings and creative mind, and a determination that one day I will be his dealer. You because he is the most exciting and unique man and lover and has moulded you into a fascinating, very sexy lady whom I have wanted to bed for a long time.'

'You overwhelm me, Ben. I had no idea you wanted me in that way,' she told him.

'I gave you many hints.'

'Ben, you and my brother are the only ones who have ever accused me of being obsessive! I'll answer you as I answered him: "So what!" Orlando's reply to that was, "Your obsession with Gideon is not healthy for either one of you." I told him that may be so, but my obsession made me the wife of one of the most exciting men in the world, and incidentally very happy. I am famous as his wife, his model, the mother of the three children he adores.'

'And?' he probed.

'I'm flattered to think you want to bed me. But you might find me as dull and boring sexually as the art world pundits think I am.'

'Not all of them,' he told her.

'I've never had an affair,' she confessed.

'That's hard for me to believe, maybe because I have for years fantasised how you and I would be together. Turn my fantasies to reality. Come to lunch at my place tomorrow.'

'An assignation in the afternoon? That in itself is exciting. I have only one reservation. We have been good friends for a very long time, I wouldn't want to lose that friendship because in a misguided moment of passion we became lovers. I will never leave Gideon.'

'I love you, Dendre, but I am not *in love* with you and I accept that you will never leave him.'

The temptation to add a lover to her life was hard to resist and she did find Ben attractive, always had. They were interrupted by a waiter changing plates and the woman on his left once again engaged him in conversation. Throughout the rest of dinner he was unable to break away from the young woman. As everyone was rising from the table to have after dinner drinks and coffee, Dendre whispered in his ear, 'Do you swear to keep it our secret?'

'If that's what you want,' he whispered back.

Just at that moment Gideon arrived and placed a kiss upon her cheek and an arm around her shoulders to take her to meet someone.

In the gallery, after several introductions, she found herself alone which was not unusual unless someone wanted to talk her into arranging an introduction to Gideon. She worked her way through the crowd and found Ben.

'Yes,' she told him.

FIRE ISLAND,
NEW YORK CITY,
HYDRA

1993

Chapter 10

'You seem far away, a little lost. May I join you?' asked one of the regulars at The Sounion.

Dendre greeted the man as he took a seat at her table. 'Tassos, how nice to see you. I was far away, drifting in time, remembering some of the highs and lows of my life.'

'Not such a good idea, Mrs Palenberg. Better to live in the present. What was, was. The good things and the bad. Now let me buy you a drink.' And he snapped his fingers for service.

Dendre placed a hand on his arm and told him, 'Thank you Tassos, wise words. I've been wallowing in the past out of pure self-indigence. But no, thank you very much for the offer but I've had a long, difficult day. What I need now is to go home.'

Dendre shook the man's hand and found Dimitri at the bar, talking politics with a group of Greek sailors. It made her smile. Reminded her that the Greeks' national pastime was talking politics and always passionately. It made her long to be in the Hydra house.

Dimitri was appalled when Dendre told him not to ring for a cab, she would walk home. 'Dressed like that, in this neighbourhood, at this hour? No,' he told her. She acquiesced, he was right, this was not Hydra or even Athens where it was safe at any time, night or day.

All the lights were on in Gideon's studio. Several in the

133

apartment above where they lived. It was three in the morning. Gideon and the girls will have been worried, especially Amber, she thought. Dendre walked up the three flights and let herself in.

Orlando, Gideon, and Adair pounced on her the moment she entered the apartment. 'Where on earth have you been? We've been worried half to death,' said Orlando.

Before Dendre could say a word, Gideon took her by the arm and ushered her into the bedroom. There he kissed her then told her, 'I was more shocked than worried not to find you here. I think this is the first time in all our married life you've not been here waiting for me. Where were you? Why did you leave the museum?'

Dendre realised then that Orlando had been right: her feeling for Gideon had been, and still was, more obsession than love. She could see it so clearly now: how she had become obsessive as a defence mechanism to keep him from leaving her. What had brought her to her senses was Gideon's open display of love for Adair, for all the world to gossip about. How he'd barely paid attention to Dendre all evening, never acknowledging her as the one woman, his wife, who enriched his life. He had accepted the immense honour he had been given with not a mention of her name when without Dendre he might never have become the great artist that he was. He knew it, Dendre knew it, and she felt the world should have been told.

They were gazing into each other's eyes. There was no love for her in Gideon's; caring possibly, maybe a little concern. She hated the look he gave her now. He had never had it before Adair had come on the scene. Dendre had seen so many women come and go in their lives: mistresses, short romances, one-night stands. When he was smitten with one there was always a portrait, and once that was finished so was the woman. With Adair it had been different right from the start. This beautiful young creature who was everything that Dendre was not had wound herself into Gideon's soul with her mind, her wit and her body. She had something special that all the others did not. Adair could talk art with the same passion and keenness as Gideon. She could and did stand up and challenge him. *She* was no one's door mat for love. Quite the opposite.

The truth was Adair had now become Gideon's chief muse; she and her bright mind were inspirational to him. She was adding a new and exciting dimension to his life. His work had a new freshness to it that drew more accolades than ever. That had always been the way with Gideon; in every new painting or sculpture, every work of art he created, there was another subtle innovation, a surge of creative passion. Something to open the mind and soul and lift one out of the mundane to rise a little higher, experience the beautiful and profound.

Dendre stepped away from him. 'I was at The Sounion. I'm surprised you didn't work that out. Why did I leave the museum? That's too complicated to go into now.'

She recognised a flash of anger on his face. 'If you have something to say about this bizarre behaviour of yours, then come out and say it.'

Orlando was right, Dendre should be cautious. She still loved her husband, whether obsessively or not, their children, the lifestyle he had given her. She knew she would have to turn her obsession back to love and herself into an exciting individual in her own right if she was still to remain Gideon Palenberg's wife.

'Your winning the Medal of Honour, the exhibition, the dinner party . . . it was spectacular. I'm afraid I was over-whelmed by it all and became emotional. My mind kept playing tricks on me and I somehow felt disorientated. That's why I left the museum and went to The Sounion.'

Relief that there was not going to be a confrontation showed on Gideon's face. He pulled her into his arms and kissed her, deeply and with passion. 'I love you. I will always love you. We've come a long way together. I'll ask Orlando to take Adair home.'

Gideon never lied, and he wasn't lying now. She knew he loved her – but for what she had been, obsessively in love with him, which at this time in his life was not enough. Together they walked from the bedroom to the drawing room and bade Adair and Orlando good night. Once in bed, still high on the evening, Gideon pulled Dendre into his arms. They were lying on their sides facing each other. She waited for a caress, some words of love, but in vain. Instead he draped one of her legs over his hip and reached between them, parted her most intimate lips and thrust forcefully into her.

All her pent-up emotion broke and she called out as she slipped into sexual bliss. Gideon drove deeply into her again and again. He moved with a slowness he knew would give her the greatest pleasure. They came together in exquisite orgasm that seemed to fire their lust. They were on another plane, lost in an erotic landscape. As Dendre and Gideon dissolved in their many orgasms they were reborn again and again, freed of their egos, nothing more than two souls in love with lust.

The following morning when he kissed her awake he did not mention the night before. She thought she saw a troubled look, an unease, in his face. Did he in spite of himself still love her? Had the sex been more than sublime? Was he as much in love with his wife as he was with Adair?

He had them both but it was Adair calling the shots, not Gideon, while Dendre played the submissive, loving wife.

She had no doubt in her mind that if she confronted Gideon about Adair, he would leave her for his mistress. Dendre saw herself as going to war to save her marriage. To do that she would have to do battle with both Gideon and Adair. Once she had worked that out a new sense of confidence took her over and she felt happy in a different way than ever before.

Dendre made breakfast for Gideon and herself: large glasses of orange juice, omelettes filled with chicken livers and mushroom, toasted brioche, apricot jam and a pot of coffee. Yukio carried it down the stairs to the studio and arranged the food on the small dining table where more often than not Gideon breakfasted alone.

Dendre followed him down the stairs and saw Gideon preparing a new canvas. Absorbed in his work, he hadn't heard them. It gave her a minute or two to study her husband. She could understand why women fell in love with him. He had such energy, the charisma of greatness seemed to ooze from every pore in his body. He had such passion. Just to meet him once was a privilege. Everyone wants to touch greatness at least once in their life and she had been living with it for thirty odd years. She did not intend that to stop. She said to herself, Move out of my life, Adair, or take the consequences.

Gideon heard his wife's laughter echoing all the way round the vast studio. He stopped his work and Yukio called out, 'Breakfast, Gideon.'

At the table he said, 'It's a long time since I heard you laugh like that. I like it when you're happy, the way you sound this morning.'

'Let's go to the Hydra house! I long for the island and the sea. Just a month or two there then straight to Fire Island for the summer?' suggested Dendre.

'I'll think about it.'

'Is it an anti-climax for you this morning after such a star-studded gala, having the world handed to you on a platter?' she asked.

'No. I feel no anti-climax. Proud maybe, a little self-satisfied, extremely happy for the recognition and the knowledge I will never have to think about money again. Nor will you or my girls.' He stopped eating for a moment and then added, 'This omelette is fantastic. I was hungry as hell. You *are* a wonder with eggs, Dendre.'

They ate in silence for several minutes, each of them lost in thought. Dendre's were about her adversary, Adair, who hated the kitchen as much as Dendre loved it. Adair could just about make coffee; Dendre was a master chef after years of cookery courses.

A plan was forming in her mind about how to rid herself of Adair and keep her husband. She conceded it was not going to be easy, but she was determined not to be depressed about having to do it. Rather to have fun being a bitch. Gideon broke the silence. Dendre felt a twinge of guilt. Being devious and assertive did not come easily to her.

'You seem a bit jumpy this morning,' he said. 'Is anything bothering you?'

'No. Let's put it down to not having enough sleep, but I'm not complaining.'

'Well, I should hope not,' said Gideon with a broad smile on his face.

'You know, we're shameless in bed for a couple who have been together so long,' she told him, returning his smile.

'Well, it isn't as if we hadn't worked on it,' he said, and immediately changed the subject. 'OK, I've thought about it long enough. Yes, we'll go to Hydra. I need a few days, a week at the most, and then we can leave. We can send Valdez and Yukio out to open the house and studio a few days before our arrival. I've been wanting to work on a series of engravings. The Hydra studio would be the perfect place to do that. I'll leave the details and arrangements to you.'

Dendre felt so happy, she was afraid she might burst with joy. She had won round one of the fight to keep her husband. She had removed him from Adair – well, at least out of her orbit. She had no illusions that Gideon would not be on the telephone to her, might even invite her to stay for a while in the house. Stumbling blocks that could be overcome one at a time.

Gideon rose from the table and said, 'The phone will be ringing all day – congratulations, interviews, the lot. You handle them. I'll see no one, I want to work. No lunch, just leave some food and I'll send up for it. Tell the girls, who will no doubt want to talk about last night, we can have a party post-mortem over dinner this evening. By the way, I was mightily proud of them. They looked sensational, and were all dressed with such panache. I do like a pretty woman.'

'I do know that, Gideon,' she said facetiously.

'Whoops!' he said and both of them had the good grace to laugh.

Valdez and Tony arrived and were given explicit instructions on mixing the paints Gideon wanted. He walked away from Dendre without another word. She took no offence; he had done that thousands of times when he was ready to immerse himself in work.

She let herself out of the studio and into the apartment. There was a great deal to do in a short period of time. She found Pieta in the bath listening to rock and roll on her headphones, Amber still asleep, and Daisy doing excercises. She told all three, 'Breakfast in twenty minutes – and I mean twenty, not forty.'

Dendre and Kitty, her helper, prepared a platter of fresh

fruit, eggs, muffins and coffee. While standing over the coddled eggs Dendre thought of what Gideon had said about how beautiful and well turned out her blonde-haired, violet-eyed daughters had been. He'd made no mention of how *she'd* looked. No more shopping for bargains at Lohman's in Brooklyn, she vowed. She was going for a new look, and for once in her life had no intention of looking at the price tags.

The last one to arrive at the table was Pieta, who remarked, 'What a spread, Mom. You must have something to say or ask for.'

Dendre looked at her three daughters whose looks and colouring resembled Gideon's side of the family. Their still developing characters were already formidable. They adored their father, his work and his fame, and took their mother a little for granted. Intelligent and sensitive girls, they were aware that they belonged to a far from typical American family but were also aware that they were a part of a close-knit one, and felt privileged as a result of that.

Gideon and Dendre were proud of their three girls because not once had they taken advantage of their father's fame. From toddlers they had been exposed to all sorts of people in the art world and especially the beautiful women who would float in and out of their home. When they were old enough to realise that their father had lovers, it had been Gideon who had sat all three of them down and told them, 'You must be like your mother is about these ladies who come and go in my life. Accepting, never questioning, befriending them, enjoying what they have to offer, then forgetting them. They are outside how I feel about your mother and you girls. She has never mentioned or complained about my dalliances, and that is very clever of her. You must do the same. End of subject forever. And you are not to talk about this to your mother. It would embarrass her and I won't have that.'

There had been a certain commanding tone in their father's voice then. It said, This is my life, and your mother's. Don't question it or else! The three girls made a pact never to interfere with their parent's lifestyle. They respected their mother for loving their father enough to leave him his freedom. Their father for having been so honest and telling them how to handle his infidelities while at the same time teaching them there are different ways and reasons to love.

'Did you ever see such a gala evening as last night? And what happened to you, Mom? We were all so worried when we didn't know where you were. Then Adair said not to be, she saw you go off with Haver and his crowd, so we went to bed. Did you go off with Haver? You should have come with us. We went dancing at some new place Adair found. Sort of a dump but the music was great.'

'Didn't the women look chic? And that dress Adair was wearing – wow!' said Daisy.

'Was Pieta right? Do you have something on your mind, Mom? God, these eggs are great. Are there any of those tiny sausages?'

Dendre went to the oven and took the sausages to the table to the sound of her chattering daughters reliving the night before. She placed the covered dish on the table. Daisy jumped from her chair and went to kiss her mother on the cheek.

'Mom, you never forget anything! You're the best in the world.'

Amber repeated, 'Is Pieta right, Mom, is there something you want to tell us?'

Dendre began to laugh. 'Yes, I do, *and* ask you something as well.'

'Well, what are you waiting for, Mom? We're all ears,' said Amber.

Dendre laughed. 'I was waiting for the three of you to stop stuffing your faces.'

'Mom, we *are* capable of listening and eating at the same time. But wait one minute, I'll just get the damson jam . . .'

When Amber returned to the table, Dendre asked, 'How about Easter on Hydra? Your father and I are leaving some time during this coming week. We intend to stay there until the end of June and go straight on to Fire Island.'

There were mumbles through mouthfuls of food.

'Great.'

'Can I bring Sam Wong and Jessie along?' asked Amber,

'I'd like to bring Isobel,' said Pieta.

The other two cried out, 'No!'

'Your father will be annoyed if you bring Isobel. She clings to him and gets so starry-eyed, and her aspirations to be a painter irritate him because she has no talent. I think not, Pieta.'

She pouted and complained, 'I never, ever get what I want!'

Dendre and her other two daughters burst out laughing because Pieta, being the youngest, got everything she wanted more often than not. Daisy, who was sitting next to her, leaned over and began tickling and teasing her. 'Oh, poor baby. Little hard-done-by Pieta. Orphan Annie.'

She convulsed with laughter, screaming, 'Stop! Oh, please stop, please!'

'Admit that Isobel is a crashing bore and I will,' said Daisy.

'She is, she is, I give up!'

Daisy stopped and Pieta wiped the tears of laughter from her cheeks. After finally catching her breath she said, 'She really is but I have a crush on her brother.'

A resounding, 'Get a crush on someone else!' came from

the three others at the table. Everyone including Pieta laughed.

The girls were used to moving from house to house, it was a way of life for them and always an adventure. When they had been younger there had been tutors to make up for time missed at school. They were a family who liked to live together, enjoyed each other's company better than anyone else's. There was no place more exciting than where their mother and father were. Dendre was the centre of the world for them, always there nurturing her brood, her husband, their friends.

'Well, up goes the phone bill,' said Amber. The girls called at least three times a week to talk to their parents when they were not all together.

That was the easy part, thought Dendre.

She poured herself another cup of coffee and while doing so asked, 'How would you like to go shopping with me today? No, let's say tomorrow.'

Eating came to a halt. The girls fell silent. If there was anything they dreaded it was a day spent shopping with their mother. She looked at every price tag, resented buying anything at the regular price, and always complained, 'We could have done better in Lohman's.' The girls, after a miserable day, generally managed to buy what they wanted *at regular price* but the effort invariably left them in a foul mood: not even talking to their mother. Dendre remembered the years of penury she and Gideon had suffered. Her saving grace with the girls was that she never reminded them of the bad old days she and Gideon had been through to get where they were now, able to spoil their children with frivolous shopping sprees, no prices asked.

The three of them looked at one another in surprise because they knew how much Dendre usually detested those shopping days that should have been fun. Amber and Daisy were old enough to shop on their own now and did, but they were close to their mother and respected her opinion in spite of how difficult she made shopping. Dendre did have a style of her own which the girls thought of as inverted snobbery: no famous labels, never chic, always looking interesting rather than beautiful.

The girls felt that she was right in some ways. Dendre's aversion to famous labels and huge prices, her fear of being labelled as stylish and wealthy, kept her daughters on track. They, as the offspring of a world-famous and much celebrated artist, wanted to create a style of their own that straddled the chic of Adair and the look their mother had created: that of a poor artist's wife with long bias-cut skirts down to the ankle, worn black turtle neck jumpers, and trappings of a successful artist's wife too – Ancient Mayan gold necklaces that were more art form than jewellery, a fabulous full-length chinchilla coat.

'Your lack of enthusiasm is ringing in my ears. Will answers come easier if I tell you I am throwing out all my clothes and starting afresh? The spree is for me not for any of you, and money's no object,' Dendre told her girls.

None of them spoke until Daisy, in slow motion, slid down in her chair and fell to floor in a make-believe faint. The three still sitting at the table and Daisy on the floor burst into peals of laughter.

'I need your help, girls. I'll never get anywhere on my own and your father said you three looked the best of anyone at the gala, the most glamorous and enchanting. I have never looked glamorous or enchanting. I think I would like to.'

'Mom, what's this in aid of? Why now? Are you making this change for Dad?' asked Amber.

'No, I'm doing it for me.'

Pieta ran to her mother and plunked herself down on Dendre's lap. She kissed her and said, 'You're better looking than Barbra Streisand, and look what she made out of herself!'

'I'll take that as a compliment, dear, thank you.'

Daisy said, 'Of course we'll go with you. What fun it will be!'

'We'll definitely go with you, Mom. I wouldn't miss this for the world. Does Dad know about the new look?' asked Amber.

'No. It's not that it's a secret, just let's say I don't see the need to make a big thing out of going shopping.'

'Do you want to go today? We can make it, can't we, Pieta, Daisy? It's going to be such fun,' enthused Amber.

Before the girls could answer, Dendre said, 'Not today. I thought I would go to Elizabeth Arden for my hair and the right way to make up, then get the clothes to match my makeover.'

'I'll go with you,' said Amber.

The others offered to go too but Dendre declined their help.

The girls said they would stay away from Elizabeth Arden's Salon on Fifth Avenue if she would treat them to tea and cakes at the Russian Tea Room afterwards. Dendre agreed on one condition: that the girls should not discuss this outing with their father or Adair.

'I want to introduce the new me into our life as unobtrusively as possible.'

The girls agreed. But Dendre could see by the looks on their face that they understood something was amiss to have brought about such a radical change in their mother. They respected Dendre enough to have the good grace not to pry any further. For them, it was enough to be included in her escapade.

The girls returned to their food and Dendre called Yukio and Kitty to the table. Yukio was to man the phones and work on their travel plans. Kitty was given instructions on how to cook the evening's dinner as Dendre explained that she expected to be out all day. The cleaner-cum-cook looked astounded. For the first time in all the years Kitty had been with the Palenbergs, Dendre had entrusted the entire meal to her.

Chapter 11

Dendre was on her way to Elizabeth Arden when she pulled out her mobile telephone and called the salon to say she would be half an hour late. Although she had a vague plan in her mind of how to get rid of Adair and win back her husband, she was very much dependent on instinct as to when and how to move forward. It was therefore as much of a surprise to her as it was to Adair when Gideon's mistress opened the door of her penthouse flat to see Dendre standing in the hall.

Her initial idea had been to get herself made over first and then confront Adair but in the taxi going to the salon she thought that seemed somehow pathetic. She rationalised that getting all dressed up like some dowager duchess might make Adair think she was trying to compete with the younger woman's chic and good looks, which was not the case. Dendre was no fool. She knew that with all the money in the world spent on hairdressers, beauty therapists, cosmeticians, and clothes, she would still lose. Hence the change of plan. She wanted Adair to see that any changes in Dendre's life were for her own sake and not made to compete with Adair or anyone else.

'Good morning,' she said with a smile, noticing how beautiful Adair looked, hair tousled from sleep, without make-up, wearing silver crêpe-de-Chine pyjamas.

'Dendre, what's wrong?' she asked, face full of fear.

147

'What a surprise! I would have guessed you wore sexy black satin night dresses rather than jim-jams,' said Dendre, a note of bitchiness in her voice.

'Only when I sleep with your husband,' was the snappy retort.

'Aren't you going to invite me in?' she asked.

'Of course, come in. For heaven's sake, Dendre, is Gideon all right?'

Dendre entered the apartment and said, 'Yes, of course he's all right!' a note of irritation in her voice.

There was a huge sigh of relief from Adair who placed the palm of her hand over her heart, the fear fading away from her face. 'Oh, Dendre, you so frightened me. Come into the kitchen, I was just having a cup of coffee. Would you like one?'

There had always been between Adair and Dendre a civilised acceptance of each other's position. Both of them in the past had worked hard not to offend the other. Each had been put in a precarious position: one wrong move on either woman's part and Gideon would be rid of them in a shot.

Adair had been a part of Dendre's life for the last two years: a constant visitor, a threesome with her husband when the children were not with them. They travelled together, were quasi-friends, not by choice but by Gideon's will that they should be. Both women had learned their place and not to offend the other. Each had found a way to live peaceably within their love triangle, mostly by ignoring each other.

In the kitchen, Adair took over. While pouring a cup of coffee for Dendre she said, 'What's going on? It's not like you to turn up at my door. Does Gideon know you're here? Why didn't he come with you?'

'I want you to promise me you'll not say a word to him about this visit?'

'I would be lying if I gave that promise to you,' answered Adair.

'Too bad. It will be as dangerous for you as it will for me if you don't. But it really doesn't matter all that much. I've made up my mind to get rid of you, once and for all. I'm reclaiming my husband, no matter what the cost nor the time it takes to do it. I will make this short but not sweet, Adair – I want you to leave Gideon. Dump him in the same way you dump every man you're finished with: mercilessly.'

'You're dreaming, Dendre! Or maybe you're having a midlife crisis. It could be no more than the menopause. Gideon will never leave me.'

'Oh, I know that. I saw it last night. That's why *you* have to leave *him*.'

'How stupidly naive of you, Dendre. What did you think – that all you had to do was come here and ask for Gideon and I would hand him back to you? He and I are more in love with each other than ever we have been. There isn't a day goes by when we don't talk to each other several times or make love in one way or another: a gift, a profession of love and adoration, an exchange of two minds coming together with thrilling, inspiring ideas. And then there is the sexual attraction between us. I really am sorry you lost your husband, Dendre. I know how I would feel if Gideon walked out on me.

'You married a man in ten million, maybe a billion, then got lost in the kitchen trying to keep him with a pot and a pan. You became a housekeeper, a drudge, a keeper, a sexual slave. Oh, yes, I know all about that. You had it all and forgot to step from the house into the limelight as an equal in your own right with one of the greatest artists of the twentieth century. You're Brooklyn from your shoes up and Gideon has had it with being tied down by your obsession with seeing him a family man who paints.'

Dendre turned to walk from the kitchen. Adair went after her and stopped her, grabbing her arm. 'Some of what I said was cruel but all of it is true. You've blinded yourself to it. Leave things as they are or you'll lose Gideon, I know that for a fact. I wanted your husband and I got him. Along with him came a wife and three terrific daughters, and that suits me just fine. I am not one of those women who seeks to break up a family. I have no desire to marry Gideon. Yes, it's true I would like to live with him all the time, and if he leaves you I will. But as a free woman in love, not a wife.'

'So you think! I'm not so much of a fool as not to know how convenient it is for both you and Gideon that he doesn't leave me. It was pointed out to me recently that he has always had a love-hate relationship with me. That's because I give him everything he wants and always have. He craved a woman whose only object in life was to love him, nourish him, deal with the mundane things that fill our lives and drain away the creative impulse. And he craved an ideal lover.

'He hates the fact that I am bourgeois, deadly middle class, because that's what he has fought against all his life. But when I bring him down to my level, he's comfortable, safe, loved. It doesn't matter to me whether he slips into his family mode for five minutes or five days. He needs a home base and time to gather his strength. I made that home for him, it gives him a balance in his life, and he loves me for that.

'He taught me everything he could in order to keep what we have together. Gideon saw my potential and grabbed it. He made of me a truly passionate erotic woman and he loves me for that. I'm still able to stir him sexually, and he both loves and hates me for that. So do me the courtesy of not telling me who I am and why my husband has affairs with other women. Why he is in love with you and would leave me if either one of us disturbs the status quo of this love triangle.'

'If you know all that then why are you trying to rid yourself of me? It makes no sense.'

'Because he loves me more than he and you think he does. Because I have made up my mind that I have been humiliated for the last time by you and Gideon. Because you and he flaunted yourselves as the great artist and his young, more beautiful, clever, sexy mistress as opposed to his dull, socially inadequate wife. Oh, don't look at me that way. Did you really think me as blind, dumb and weak as I pretended to be? Didn't you ever ask yourself how I was able to keep a marriage together with Gideon for so many years? No, not all that dumb, Adair.'

'The mouse that roars. Yes, I did think you dumb, a timid mouse of a woman. You're quite an actress, Dendre. You fooled not only me but the world of art as well.'

'More fool you and the art world then! Look, Adair, I didn't come here to say as much as I have, merely to demand that you dump my husband or take the consequences. If you don't go, I will leave him. He'll be free to marry you then and you can be sure he will, no matter how much you tell me you don't want him as your husband. You see, Gideon both loves and hates being married, but I can assure you he loves it more than he hates it.

'As his wife, you will lose your identity as I did. His power will draw you away from yourself and you'll get lost in being his muse, lover, confidante, critic, housekeeper, mother of his children. You don't cook – you'll learn to cook. Bad on accounts – you'll learn to keep them. Entertain – well, I suppose you will do that better than I ever did but you won't be good at running three houses and three studios. His months of seclusion and need for space? You'll have to tread a narrow line between when to move and not to move for as you know he tolerates no interference when he's working. Slowly your marriage will fall apart and you will lose him because, unlike me, you will put yourself first and compete with him for who will wear the crown.

'No, I think you would do well to leave Gideon as I ask you to or you will pay heavily for taking him away from me, Adair.'

Dendre, who ordinarily would have been depressed and insecure after a confrontation with Adair, hardly knew herself. She was more determined than ever to be rid of her rival, amazed at her own strength and determination and with no doubt that she would go to any extreme to win back her husband.

She turned on her heel and walked towards the door. Adair followed her. 'We will never give each other up, Dendre. You're making the biggest mistake of your life.'

She didn't even bother to reply, opening the door and ringing for the lift. When it arrived Dendre stepped in, and the two women glared at each other as the lift doors were closing.

Dendre looked at her wristwatch. The entire confrontation had taken fifteen minutes. 'Not bad. That gives me fifteen minutes to spare,' she said aloud.

Standing on the pavement in front of the glossy red door of the Fifth Avenue Elizabeth Arden beauty salon, the mass of people on the move up and down the avenue and streaming round her gave Dendre not a moment of hesitation but rather a super-charge of adrenalin. It was so exhilarating: all these people going somewhere, doing something, serious shoppers looking for a bit of gloss to finish themselves off so they might display themselves as something they were not but wanted to be. What was so amusing to Dendre was that with a snap of her fingers she, Dendre Moscowitz Palenberg, had become one of them. She was helpless to stop herself from laughing.

Not one person looked at her, stopped to enquire as to what was so funny. New Yorkers were used to street crazies, accepted them as part of the landscape. They were too busy minding their own business to be concerned with someone else's, even for a laugh. The uniformed doorman stepped in front of Dendre, gave her a snobbish look of surprise that such a woman as she was entertaining the thought of a session at Arden's. Nevertheless he opened the door for her and Dendre stepped into another world. Her first thoughts were, This is whipped cream, pink and silver frosting, velvet ribbon, ostrich feathers, Attar of Roses, violets and lilies of the valley.

She was dazzled as Elizabeth Arden's dictum 'beauty salon heaven makes you a delicious female' wrapped itself around her. Not a thing had been done to her, she hadn't even shed her fur-collared leather coat or slipped off her flat-heeled shoes, and yet the magic had begun. She felt pretty.

Through a maze of pale aquamarine, white, diaphanous peach and silver night gowns and negligées on display, a tall slender woman of Dendre's age approached her. She was impressive with her black hair, pale skin and ruby red lips, dressed from tip to toe in one of the smart little black suits that chic New York women were famous for wearing ever since Mainbocher had dressed Wallis Simpson.

'Mrs Palenberg, how nice to see you again. Ah, you don't remember me? We met briefly at an opening at the Metropolitan Museum of Art several years ago,' said the manageress of the salon.

Dendre nearly jumped when the woman snapped her fingers and broke the uncanny silence of the ground floor. The receptionist nodded her head and used the telephone.

As if by magic the lift appeared and the doors slid open. Margo Perriwhistle slipped her hand under Dendre's elbow and walked with her to the lift.

'I understand this is your first time here at Arden's and you have asked for advice and treatment?' asked Margo.

'Yes.'

'Have you anything particular in mind?'

'No, I want to hear what your people have to say. I've come here with an open mind, looking for serious change.'

The lift doors opened and the two women stepped from it. Dendre was once more aware of the silence, the soft lights so flattering to any woman, the thick carpets underfoot. A flurry of stunningly pretty assistants with lovely figures dressed in pale pink uniforms that made them look more like nurses than beauty therapists appeared to sweep Dendre and Margo wordlessly through the salon and into a private room that was Dendre's for the day. The pink and peach colours, soft lights, thick carpet and no windows, made Dendre feel slightly nauseous. For one brief moment she very nearly bolted from its luxurious confines.

Margo looked closely at Dendre as did every one of the therapists that arrived. The more they took her over, the more lost she felt. The make-up artist arrived with Eduardo the hairdresser. He clasped her hair in his hand and ran his fingers through the long black curly tresses. He placed his hands on her shoulders and, looking into the mirror, smiled at her. There was warmth in his touch and kindness in his eyes, and suddenly Dendre realised she was safe in his hands.

'Excuse me,' he told her, 'but your hair is some mess. Too, too long. Too dry. We have to get rid of the strands of grey, so that means colour. Too thick, and you've got split ends though those will be gone with the cut. Your eyebrows too, too heavy . . .'

'I've never tweezed my eyebrows . . .' She was prevented from continuing.

'What, never! Well, it's time you did. You've got an interesting face but you don't do anything with it,' said Garry the make-up expert.

Looking at herself surrounded by a number of beauty therapists and the daunting Margo, all but rubbing their hands with glee at such a challenge as she, Dendre swung round on the swivel chair to face them.

'I have a few things to say to you all. I need your help, desparately, but I do not want to walk out of this salon looking like mutton dressed as lamb. Nor do I want to look like I've been dipped in gloss, or spend several hours a day, every day, being groomed. I want to look stunningly attractive but with a style that is all mine, not Elizabeth Arden's. That would not reflect who and what I am. OK, I think that's all I have to say. I'm in your hands now.'

Margo looked as if she had been slapped in the face. Eduardo and Garry stood there smiling at each other and then applauded her. The nurse-like therapists averted their eyes from Margo and remained silent and still as statues. The manageress recovered from the shock of meeting a client with a mind of her own, and quite suddenly a smile crept over her face.

'Well, now we have something to work towards. I can assure you, Mrs Palenberg, you will walk from this salon happy with what you see in the mirror,'

That was when the serious work began.

The three Palenberg girls were not anxious about their mother being late as she had called the Russian Tea Room to say she would be. They did, however, keep their eyes on the door. They were rewarded with the sight of several famous faces, even a few who knew the girls and came over to greet them and congratulate them on their father's award. There was a stack of newspapers on the empty seat at their table. Large photographs of their father alone, with the President, with all three of them and with Adair made every front page.

'Look!' said Pieta.

The other two stared at the woman who had just entered the restaurant. Dendre waved to them. Speechless, they rose from their seats to wave back.

'I can't believe how beautiful she looks,' said Amber.

'She's cut her hair and it shines – it's *so* silky,' enthused Daisy.

'And what about that outfit she's wearing? Wow!' Pieta exclaimed.

By that time Dendre had arrived at their table. The girls greeted her with endless compliments and for the moment forgot the newspapers which had automatically been picked up and placed on the floor.

'Mom, everyone in the room is looking at you. You're stunning! Why ever didn't you do this before? Did you have a good time? Aren't you thrilled? Wait until Dad sees you!'

A laughing Dendre said, 'One question at a time. I didn't do it before because having to be stunning was not a priority in my life. I hadn't the time nor the money nor the inclination to make an impression on anyone except your father who loved me as I was. I never cared how I appeared to others. I never had the vanity to pamper myself as I have done today. I never had an innate understanding of style, until Louise Nevelson took me aside one day and told me how to dress up my clothes with pre-Columbian gold jewellery and glamorise myself with full-length fur coats, as she did.

'You asked, did I have a good time? I must confess I did, tedious and boring as the whole process of beautifying oneself is. I think the best of it was being pampered and made a fuss of, other people working to make me look special. By the time I'd paid the huge bill, I had a new perception of myself. Not only did they make me look special, I felt for the first time like a special lady and liked myself for that.

'Am I thrilled with the way I look? I would have to say, yes. I like my hair shoulder-length, and that all I will have to do is wash it, shake it out, and let it dry naturally. I really like the colour. I always hated those strands of grey. But no foundation and powder for me – a naked face save for eyes outlined to look larger, blusher and a perfect red lipstick. This is the new me: low-maintenance, interesting rather than chic, definitely subtle.'

'Wait until Adair sees you,' breathed Amber.

'Yes, she will be surprised,' answered her mother dryly.

'And where did you get those sensational leather trousers? Wow, do they show your figure!'

'Must have cost you a bomb. I can't believe you didn't tremble when you signed the cheque, Mom,' said Pieta with a broad smile.

The jacket Dendre was wearing was made of the same leather, a cognac colour with revers of white Persian lamb and lined with the same fur. It finished tight to the waist and on her feet were a pair of black leather ankle boots with Cuban heels. It surprised Dendre that she didn't feel flash or overdressed. She owed that to Eduardo who had whispered in her ear, 'From here you go to Gucci. There's a friend of mine there – Mario. I'll call and tell him you'll be in the shop before they close. But don't let Margo know, she'd fire me on the spot!'

'I think that the most difficult part was walking into Gucci, and not looking at a price tag,' said Dendre, quite seriously.

All three girls laughed at their mother and Daisy said, 'The same old Mom in new clothing! even if she did have to bite the bullet first. I hope you're going to shop the same way tomorrow as you did today?'

'Oh, you may be sure of that,' Dendre told her.

She very nearly gave her game away then to the girls, which she really did not want to do. She was after all certain they would see her go through many more changes besides a new hair-do, plucked eyebrows and a new wardrobe before she had won their father back for good.

The four of them settled down when the second pot of tea arrived with more cakes. Pieta picked the newspapers off the floor and handed them to her mother with a smile. Conversation turned once more to the gala evening of the night before.

Dendre thought the photographs were marvellous. Her heart beat with pride to see them. She had no feelings of jealousy because she had not been included in them, only a touch of anger that Adair had. It was Daisy who told her mother that it was such a pity Dendre had not remained with them during the evening because then she would have been in the photographs too. She read one report after the other as the girls jabbered on, only half-listening to them. They were smart and sophisticated young women and yet with the kind of innocence too that comes only with youth. Neither she nor Gideon had ever pushed them in any way and yet they had found their place and were happy in it. Each of them seemed to understand they were the most privileged of children to be the daughters of such a great man and were generous, kind, and unquestioning of their parents' unusual lifestyle. They merely made the most of it.

'I love you girls and Dad with all my heart. All of you have given me the best life a woman could ask for. I promise it will always be that way, so remember that, no matter what.

'Now let's go home. We're very late and Gideon will be wondering where we are. We're having rib of beef for dinner, medium rare,' said Dendre with a smile.

Chapter 12

Only when the taxi pulled up to the curb did Dendre think about her confrontation that morning. Had Adair or had she not told Gideon about the visit? Had she taken to heart Dendre's warning of what would happen if she didn't walk out of her relationship with Gideon?

All that was going through her mind when she heard Amber say, 'I can't wait to see Dad's face when he sees you, Mom.'

'And Adair's and Haver's,' murmured Daisy.

The girls began to scramble out of the taxi. Dendre held out her arm to block the way. 'Wait! I have a favour to ask. Two favours, actually. I want to be alone with your father when he sees the new me. And I want you to promise not to make too much of a fuss about how I look. I'd find it embarrassing.'

What she told them was true but she was also worried in case Adair had called or visited Gideon and told him about her morning visit from Dendre. She wanted to spare the girls a potentially shocking scene: their father's fury with her for disturbing the status quo and disrupting their lives.

There were protests from her daughters but they finally agreed. The four of them stood on the pavement while Dendre paid the taxi driver. When she turned around, she saw the delight and pride in their faces at what she had done with herself.

It was Pieta who said, 'Mom, what about raving about you behind your back? Surely that's permissible?'

Their sweetness touched her deeply. 'Yes, behind my back, I think I can live with that.'

It was dark out. The lights burning in Gideon's studio meant he was still there. The girls went up to the apartment and Dendre used her key to enter the studio. She felt a surge of excitement, not at all self-conscious as she'd imagined she might be. Her timing could not have been more perfect. Valdez was cleaning brushes. Gideon, smoking a large Havana cigar and holding a coffee mug containing vintage Krug, was sitting in front of the painting he had been working on all day, considering it.

Valdez heard her and looked up from his work. She approached him and put one hand on his shoulder in greeting. He smiled and nodded his approval. Dendre smiled back and continued walking towards her husband.

Gideon turned to see who was in the studio. Dendre was still some distance from him. She smiled as she continued towards him. With his eyes still on his wife, he picked the champagne bottle up off the floor and refilled his mug. He rose from his chair and walked towards her.

He handed her the mug and said, 'Dendre, you've come a long way since the day I picked you up from that bench in Washington Square. Just when I believe I know you – how you think, how you feel – you surprise me. Sometimes, like now, confound me. You look marvellous!' He walked around her before kissing her and saying, 'Thank you.'

He touched her hair then caressed it with the palm of his hand. She took a long drink of the wine and handed him back the mug. He finished what was left, placed the mug on the floor and took her in his arms to give her a hug. With his arm around her waist, they walked through the studio and up stairs to the apartment.

Dendre could not have been more pleased with her husband's reaction to her new appearance. It was an affirmation to her that he loved her as she had looked before and would love her as she was now. If that were not true he would have made more of a fuss than he had. From the way he had received her it was evident that Adair had not told him about their meeting. Was she in fact going to leave him? Dendre's heart raced with hope that this was the case.

At the top of the spiral staircase that led from the studio to the apartment Gideon placed his hands on her bottom, not in a lascivious way but in more of an affectionate, admiring way, and asked, 'What's for dinner?'

'Shrimp mousse, rib of beef just the way you like it, potatoes and red onions roasted in olive oil and balsamic vinegar with sprigs of fresh thyme. A green salad of lamb's tongue and rocket. Oh, and caramelised oranges for pudding.'

Gideon laughed. 'Do you remember how we lived for years on hand outs of your mother's heavy Jewish cooking and never had the courage, any more than Orlando did, to tell her to lighten the meals? Well, you've brought us a long way from those days too. Everyone including your husband, enjoys dining at your table enormously.'

His charm, charisma, his love for her, were all still there. Why could he not have acknowledged her to the world, confessed his love and admiration for her in some way the night before? she asked herself. And then answered honestly, Because he loves Adair more. She leaned forward and kissed her husband chastely on the cheek, then opened the door to the apartment.

As they stepped from the studio balcony into the deserted

entrance hall, he said, 'Oh, nearly forgot, there will be two more for dinner.'

'Who's coming?' asked Dendre.

'Haver called and invited himself, and I bumped into Adair and she asked if she could come.'

Bumped into Adair? Nothing had changed! He was still playing discrete so as to hurt her the least he could do under the circumstances. Now she knew for sure that Adair had not told Gideon about Dendre's demand. Instead they had gone to bed and had sex. She was now more determined than ever to rid herself of Adair Corning.

The flat was very quiet, the girls obviously in their rooms. In their bedroom Gideon announced he was going to take a shower and began undressing, leaving his clothes all over the room. Once naked he had a habit of retracing his steps, picking them up again and hanging them in their proper place.

Dendre watched him as she was taking off her jacket. She knew his every habit and loved him for them. They were such little things: the way he removed his clothes, or turned on the shower in the bathroom to warm it while he shaved. Just little things that made up their life together. She had seen these habits thousands of times and wanted to see them thousands of times more. She felt again the pain of loving her husband. It hurt her so much to think he didn't feel the same way for her, never had. Then she found strength from deep within herself and blocked out her love for him. Her determination to proceed with her plan sharpened.

She turned from the cupboard to come face to face with Gideon, watching her from the bathroom doorway. She walked to her dressing table and opened the drawer where she kept her jewellery. Dendre clasped a magnificent Mayan gold necklace round her neck and slipped several gold bangles over her hands. She thought of Mario who had suggested she dress tonight in the see-through brown silk blouse he had talked her into buying to go with her pre-Columbian jewellery. She admired herself in the mirror though she hardly knew who she was looking at. Finally Dendre rose from her chair and turned round to face Gideon who still had not moved.

He smiled at her. 'There aren't many women who after twenty-five years with me and three children could wear that blouse. I admire your audacity. No, I applaud your breasts,' he said with a smile then turned to go into the shower.

'Watch out, Adair,' Dendre said softly to herself.

She walked into the kitchen, greeting Kitty and Yukio who were sitting at one end of the massive table preparing the salad. On seeing her, Yukio rose from his chair. Kitty merely gasped. Dendre couldn't help laughing, delighted by their reaction.

'Dendre, you look magnificent,' said Yukio.

'Oh, Dendre, I don't know what to say except I agree with Yukio. It's you, I would know you anywhere, but a glamorous you.' And Kitty rose from her chair and came to hug her.

Kitty and Yukio had been with the Palenbergs for many years. They were like family, travelled with them, sat at table with them unless they were entertaining. They were confidants to their bosses and the children. They had seen many changes, had endured many shocks and surprises during the time they had been working for the family. It was a liberal household and they loved their employers and the children, the fame that rubbed off Gideon and on to them. It was therefore not unusual for Kitty to be so intimate with Dendre, nor for Yukio, who walked around her and took the apron from her hand.

'It's wonderful, isn't it?' Dendre said to her two admirers.

'Astonishing that you've done it,' said Yukio, and to himself added, I wonder why?

'And I'm going shopping with the girls tomorrow,' she told them, joy in her eyes and voice.

A groan from Yukio. Everyone knew one of those bad-tempered days was inevitable when Dendre shopped with her daughters.

'No, it's not going to be like that, Yukio. I've turned over a new leaf. It will hurt, but I'll not be penny pinching tomorrow.'

'We'll see,' he said and went over to Dendre, carefully slipping her apron over her head.

The doorbell rang while she was checking the roast. She told him to lay two more places at the dining table. 'No one fancy, just Haver and Adair, so dine with us, if you like?' she offered.

That was not unusual. The staff saw the two new arrivals as part of the Palenbergs' extended family. Wrapped in her apron, Dendre put the finishing touches to the meal but her mind was hardly on food.

The girls seemed to be delighted with this radical change of looks and behaviour in their mother. If they had not told Yukio and Kitty about her makeover, they would certainly keep silent about it until she made her entrance and took Haver and Adair by surprise. That they'd arrived together was not unusual. They adored each other, were each other's confidants. It was Daisy who let them in, Dendre could tell by the voices.

'Yukio, champagne in the drawing room,' she told him.

Daisy arrived in the kitchen. 'Mom, I stopped Haver from coming in to say hello. You must make an entrance – and for once without an apron on. I can't wait to see their faces!'

'Nor can I,' she told her daughter who was busy untying her apron strings.

'No, Daisy. I have a few things more to do in the kitchen

166

then I'll be in.' She kissed her daughter and fluffed up her hair. 'Your hair needs more movement in it,' she said quite seriously.

'I don't believe what I'm hearing! *You* talking about hair instead of soufflés!' And everyone in the kitchen burst into laughter.

Twenty minutes later, Dendre made her grand entrance into the drawing room. The girls and Gideon were marvellous, behaving as if there was nothing unusual about the way she looked. It was difficult to tell who was more flabbergasted, Adair or Haver. There was no doubt Dendre looked simply stunning in her leather trousers and the chocolate brown long-sleeved blouse that showed her breasts and nipples, made even more sensational as a look because of her pre-Columbian jewellery.

Her appearance brought Haver to his feet. Adair didn't move. Dendre was gazing directly into her eyes. She saw anger in them before Adair blushed crimson. It was she who broke the silence.

'Gideon, you should have warned me that Dendre has seen fit to change her image at this late stage in her life. I might have died of shock! As it is I'm speechless with admiration for this dramatic change but riddled with curiosity as to why she has taken such an unprecedented step. Why have you, Dendre?'

It was not difficult to detect the acid in Adair's voice. It quite shocked the girls who adored her. They had expected praise for their mother's new look, admiration of how stunningly good-looking she was this evening.

It was Pieta who in all innocence said, 'Everyone at the Russian Tea Room turned their head to look at Mom. She's at least as elegant and stylish as Barbra Streisand now, don't you think, Adair?'

'I've never liked Barbra's looks, Pieta. No matter what she does, a bad nose is a bad nose, don't you think?'

One could not help but catch the venom in Adair's barb. Always protective of Dendre, Gideon shot a look of disapproval at his beautiful mistress with her perfect nose. 'It seems your new look is taken as some sort of challenge by our lovely Adair. Is that what it is, Dendre? It shouldn't be since you have been in altogether different leagues all your lives.'

As always he was being protective of his wife when he thought she was out of her depth. Only this time she didn't feel she was. Throughout the time Adair had been with Gideon this was the first occasion on which she had broken the unwritten law: 'Never offend the wife'.

Adair sensed she had made a mistake with Gideon and was quick to back down. She rose from the sofa and went to Dendre, kissing her on the cheek before saying, 'I always thought you had a highly individual style of your own and now you have reinvented yourself. You look stunning – handsome, interesting, and with a new kind of glamour that suits you.'

Dendre knew that her adversary was being decidedly condescending towards her but wanted no more bitterness to creep into the evening. If it did, Adair would get the better of her since the young woman was far more quick and clever than she was.

'That's very generous of you to say so, Adair. Now, if you will all excuse me, I must get back to the kitchen. Gideon, will you choose the wines? Amber, you do the seating arrangements and all go to the dining table.'

Dinner was as ever superb. They became caught up in their discussion of the night before, even Dendre. Everyone ate and drank too much. Gideon and Adair sat next to each other and it was difficult not to miss his passion for the young woman: she amused him and teased him, made him laugh constantly.

He wanted her so badly, always touching her under cover of a jest or to make a point.

Finally, the meal over, they rose from their chairs and lingered, talking about the Henry Moore bronze reclining nude that was the centrepiece on the dining table and had been lit by small round church candles. It was then that Dendre took Adair by the arm and said, 'Do come and see my jacket, I'd like your opinion of it.'

It was a bald-faced lie and the two women knew it. Dendre had been clever in asking Adair when Gideon was standing next to her. He beamed with pleasure and slid his arm from his mistress's.

In the bedroom Adair said, 'Well, let's see that blasted jacket we both know was just an excuse for you to get me alone.'

'You didn't tell Gideon about my visit?'

'Well, obviously not,' she answered testily.

'And are you going to leave him?' asked Dendre with more hope than belief.

'Most certainly not! Leave it alone, Dendre, if you want to keep him. He's ready to leave you for me, I promise that's the truth. One false move is all it will take.'

'I won't stop in my quest to get you out of our lives, Adair.'

'Oh, please! You are so naive sometimes I despair of you, Dendre. A new set of clothes and a hair-do to impress Gideon isn't going to get you what you want.'

'You think I did this for Gideon? Quite wrong. I did it for me. Has he told you we're off to the Hydra house for the next few months?'

'When?' asked Adair.

'Oh, then you didn't know? I told him I wanted to go, he thought about it and we're going on Friday.'

'You did that deliberately, to separate us! You knew it would be difficult for me to get away because of my commitments at the Metropolitan Museum. You've become more devious than I ever imagined you could be.'

'Needs must.'

'Now I *will* tell him everything.'

'Better think of the consequences first,' warned Dendre.

'And so should you!'

'Oh, I have.'

With that Dendre went to the wardrobe and took out the jacket to her suit, slipping it on. 'Now you've seen it,' she said and walked away, leaving Adair behind. Her rival sat on the bed for several minutes trying to come to terms with Dendre's sudden determination to be rid of her.

Dendre walked into the drawing room and announced, 'I feel like The Sounion. How about it, Haver?'

'I'm for it,' he answered.

'Gideon?'

'That's a great idea. Girls, get your coats. Oh, wait a minute, Adair hates the place. Well, she's outvoted. We'll go. Where is she anyway?'

'Here. What's happening?' she replied as she entered the room.

'Dendre's had a brilliant idea – we're going to round off the evening at The Sounion,' said Haver.

'If I'm outvoted I suppose I'll have to go even though I detest everything about the place. No! I can't face it. I'd rather have an early night.'

'I'll call you a taxi,' said Gideon.

The fast boat from Piraeus to Hydra had but a few people on it: several Americans and half a dozen Hydriots, all of whom knew Gideon and Dendre. There were hugs, welcome homes and smiling faces, ready to gossip about what had happened on the island since they had been away. Packages were opened, and pistachios and fresh fruit, were offered. Out came the bottle of ouzo.

Gideon was the island's most famous and revered celebrity and they all loved him and guarded his privacy. They respected the way he and Dendre and the children had learned Greek. It was to her they went to discuss any problem that arose between the Hydriots and the foreigners who resided there because she was fluent in the language and most of the other foreign residents were not. They often said of Gideon and Dendre, 'They not only speak Greek, they think Greek.'

The Hydriots, who were anything but subtle, remarked endlessly on how beautiful Dendre had become. They also enquired when the children and Adair were arriving, never shy to ask a question.

When the island came into view, Gideon took Dendre by the hand and they walked out of the saloon on to the deck at the prow of the ship as did most everyone else. The sun was hot, the air fresh and cool, and there was no wind, just a breeze. The perfect Greek winter's day.

'There is magic in the Greek Islands, no wonder the gods dwelt here. I have always chosen to believe they actually lived and chose to become myths so they might outlast us all,' said Gideon. With one arm round Dendre's waist he pulled her to him and kissed her passionately on the lips.

She too felt a certain magic in the islands. She and Gideon were never closer than when they were in Greece. That kiss, the way he feels towards me now, is a love he will never have for Adair. Unfortunately he's blinded to that and lost in his passion for her. The only way he will ever squarely face his love for me, beyond Adair or any other women, is once I'm gone, Dendre told herself.

They watched the island grow larger as they drew closer. Gideon and Dendre gazed at one other. Excitement showed in their faces, pure joy. It made them laugh and Dendre grabbed Gideon and kissed him passionately, first on the lips and then on his cheeks, nose and chin. He picked her up by the waist and sat her on the ship's rail. She managed to turn herself round and drop her legs over it. Protests from the others, fearful she would fall overboard, made no impression on either Dendre or Gideon.

They were close enough to the island for her to look down into the clear water and see it looming up from the depths. The Captain blew the ship's horn three times to announce its arrival as they rounded one end of the island and the crescent-shaped harbour inched itself into view. Slowly, more and more of the port appeared until they were approaching straight on what looked like a man-made amphitheatre of sparkling white houses, climbing one above the other, higher and higher, to the top of the steep hill.

The Palenberg house was very nearly halfway up, easy to spot since it was almost dead centre of the port. It had taken years to buy the adjoining properties surrounding their original two houses. Now it was perfect, all they could ever want. It ranged over three tiers of land, one above the other, and was surrounded by high white walls. A large family house, a smaller one that Gideon and Dendre kept as their private bedroom and bathroom, a guest house, massive studio, another house for staff. There were four courtyards of potted flowering plants and herbs, three fig trees, and a swimming pool. Gideon and Dendre almost never left their compound when they were in Hydra. When they did it was to go to a restaurant, a rare occasion because Gideon preferred Dendre's cooking. It was more usual for them to go down to the port early in the morning before the shops opened and have coffee with the locals, go for a swim, or take their boat and sail for a day.

All around the port there were cafés and restaurants and shops, all deserted now because the tourist season was still months away. Dendre could see the harbour master and his assistants walking round the port to the quay where the ship was meant to dock. She spotted Yukio and Kitty among a crowd of people arriving there. Dendre waved, and they and half a dozen others waved back.

Gideon helped her off the ship's rail and together they disembarked and were greeted effusively as people swarmed around them. They had no luggage to contend with, that had all gone ahead with their staff. Gideon spotted two of his assistants, Valdez and Barry, rushing down the steep narrow cobblestone steps flanked by the white walls of the harbourside houses. They were coming from the studio. Gideon remarked to Dendre, 'There they are. I had a moment of panic when I didn't see them here. Thought they might still be fighting the customs people with the load of materials I lumbered them with.'

All the staff, Dendre and Gideon, stayed in the port drinking and eating: charcoal-grilled octopus, chunks of bread dipped in the best extra virgin olive oil and sprinkled with salt, green and black olives. A fisherman walked by with a huge grey fish and Gideon bought it and invited the man to join them for lunch, then walked across the port to give it to the cook at the restaurant he liked.

There were twenty-two at their table set on the cobblestones where they could be close to the water. Everyone drank and ate too much but they were far from being inebriated. One of the donkey boys who ran a string of animals that carried people and all sorts of things up from the port, offered Dendre a ride to her house so that was how she arrived home.

Every day that followed was a glorious Greek winter's day, the sort that travel brochures show glossy photographs of. Every night was spent in hours of gratified lust. However, Dendre felt deep down that those evenings had an undercurrent of violence, evidence of Gideon's love-hate for her. The morning following their arrival he went to work. Dendre went to her kitchen or worked on the plants with Yorgos the gardener. Her neighbours called on her with gifts of cakes or jars of preserve. She felt happy and strong. Life was bliss without Adair in it.

What started off as a wonderful time alone with Gideon ended dramatically only five days later.

Chapter 13

Gideon came in from the port with eggs still warm from the hens when he had placed them in the basket, thick slabs of ham, a huge chunk of Gruyère cheese and three loaves of bread. In a smaller basket were wild mushrooms. Dendre made a *frittata*, a sort of open omelette, and everyone living in the compound sat down to breakfast. After their meal Gideon went to his studio and everyone else back to their chores.

It was a grey day and without the sun quite chilly. All the fires were going in the fireplaces, the central heating on low. There was something rather cosy about being in an island house in these dull winter days. Dendre decided to let Kitty do the lunch and she would do the dinner. She intended to spend the morning in her bedroom reading a good book.

Gideon wanted no more than sandwiches and a thermos of black coffee in the studio. He was engrossed in drawings for the series of engravings he was working on. At lunchtime Dendre went to the kitchen and had a bowl of soup and a chunk of bread, then went back to her bedroom. It seemed such a quiet, peaceful house without the children there, no Adair or house guests, so luxurious to be alone.

It was about two in the afternoon when she saw the light flash on the telephone. It was the studio extension. The first call lasted about forty minutes, followed shortly after by a second. Gideon could be calling anyone about any number of things but she couldn't help but wonder if it was Adair to whom he was talking. It actually didn't matter if it was. Dendre intended to confront him about her on their return to New York. She wanted the next few months alone with him and the children, then she would be ready to leave him if she had to.

A matter of moments after the flashing light on the telephone was extinguished the second time Dendre picked up her book again, only to put it down as Gideon entered the bedroom.

'Hi,' he said.

'I'm loving today,' she replied.

He made no reply to that but went directly across the room to the bed and removed the collection of white hand-woven cushions. He carried them to the fireplace where he dropped them on the floor. To Dendre her husband looked inspired, full of youth and vigour. Only five days on the island and it was already working its magic. There was a look of utter bliss in his eyes and lust on his mind. It was that that made Dendre sit up on the chaise. He went to her and took her hand, pulling her into his arms, hugging then releasing her.

In that hug she sensed overwhelming love. He undressed her tenderly and spoke to her in a quiet, soft voice. 'Let's make love as no other lovers have ever done. No words to break the moment, just two people in lust and love.'

Dendre began undressing him. Her hands were trembling. Naked, they stood facing each other. He stepped in close to her and kissed her on the forehead, then the tip of her nose. He licked her lips and kissed them. With pointed tongue he licked her from her neck in a straight line down to her navel. His hands were like the finest feathers, so light were his caresses.

He took her breasts one at a time and caressed them, placed

176

his lips over her nipples and sucked them till the nimbus round them puckered. He laid her down on a cushion and himself over her and made her ready to receive him with caressing fingers grown wet with her lust.

Time and again he kept telling her, between slow and exquisite thrusting, how much he loved her. Dendre lost control of her orgasms as they came rapidly, flowing one after another, sending her into a bright cloud of sweet bliss. She whimpered, shedding tears of pure joy for being fucked by love. For it was love, not passion, nor a mere penis, governing this intercourse.

When they came together he let out a scream. 'Oh, yes! Yes, my goddess of love,' and rested prone over her body for some time before rolling off.

Dendre lay in front of the open fire and watched the leaping flames. Gideon had his eyes closed. She reached out to take his hand and he pulled it away. Dendre was shocked. He had never rejected her, ever! It was as if he had slapped her in the face and awakened her from a trance. Gideon had not made love like that to her since they were young lovers. And then the realisation hit her. He had not in fact been making love to her at all but to Adair. It came back to her: 'No words to break the moment.' Of course not. He didn't want to break the illusion with a Brooklyn accent when he was imagining he was with Adair, with her beautiful, well-educated voice.

For a few seconds Dendre thought she was going to be sick right there. She took deep breaths and tried to calm herself. When she got over the sickness, anger at having been used that way, as a surrogate fuck for Adair, overwhelmed her. It was a horrible thing for Gideon to do. He had crossed the line he himself had drawn: to hurt Dendre as little as possible under the circumstances. For all the sexual antics she and Gideon had indulged in, she had never felt ashamed or dirty before.

She did now. She felt as if she had been used like a whore, bought and paid for by a lifestyle. That she had been used and abused with no compunction whatsoever by Gideon because of her obsessive love for him.

She felt no less guilty than he for the state of their marriage: her low self-esteem, obsessive love and concealed awareness once she had grown into it. So what? Fuck feeling guilty! It's counter-productive, a waste of energy, she told herself. So she tossed that away and hung on to her anger.

Dendre climbed back into her blue jeans and slipped into the white, drop-shouldered silk blouse that had been tossed to the floor. She buttoned the balloon sleeves of the blouse tight to her wrists and was just about to slip into the sleeveless sheepskin jacket she had been wearing when Gideon opened his eyes.

'Oh, good, you're awake,' she said as she threw the handwoven, velvet-lined car rug to him.

'I'm not cold,' said Gideon who didn't much like the tone of her voice nor the look in her eye. He had never heard or seen them before.

'I didn't throw it to you because I was worried about whether you are cold or not. I simply don't want to see you lying there naked, replete with love and sex.'

'Well, that's a first,' he replied, and made no move to cover himself. 'What's this all about, Dendre?' he asked, a note of annoyance in his voice.

'You were fucking me but making love to Adair, Gideon. "Let's make love as no other lovers have ever done." You were talking to her not me. "No words to break the moment." Oh, yes, but only because you wanted to keep the illusion that the body you were making love to, having tender sex with, was your mistress's and not your wife's.'

It was then that Gideon rose from the floor and pulled on

178

his baggy jeans and paint-stained old jumper. He had never seen Dendre the way she was now. She was, of course, spot on. He walked to a table and took a cigar from the humidor, nipping the tip with a cutter he kept in his pocket. Then he walked back to the fireplace. Gideon stood there, rolling the cigar slowly between his fingers to light it evenly and taking several puffs.

Dendre had watched his every move, waiting in vain for him to say something. She was clear-thinking enough to know he would not deny her accusations. He was many things but never a liar.

'Your silence tells me it's all true. Oh, Gideon! I can tell you just how it happened. You called Adair and she told you how much she loved you, how much she wanted you. You had sex on the telephone then finally managed to say goodbye. A short time passed and you called her again, only this time your lust took over. You spoke dirty to her, she loved it and led you on. What did she say? "Put down the telephone and go fuck Dendre and make believe it's me, my love"?'

'It's pointless to go on with this. Let it drop, Dendre.'

There it was, the order and the veiled threat. 'Not this time, Gideon.'

'What do you want me to say – that I love you? You know that.'

'Yes, I do. And more than you think you do. That's why I'm asking you to give up Adair. No, I'm actually *telling* you to get her out of our lives today and forever.'

'That's impossible. I beg you, don't go on with this,' he told her as he sat down in a chair next to the hearth.

'Why? Because you think you love her more than you love me? Because you want to make another life with a younger woman?'

'Yes! And because she makes me happy, because she is

vibrant and clever and amusing and terrifyingly beautiful. She's strong, can stand up to me. And because we have so much in common. She's a brilliant art historian who understands the art world and sees it very much as I do. She's my muse and I am enriched by her love for me.

'I still love you, Dendre, we have a history of love, but it *is* history. Time has marched on. I need different things in my life, to add to it. It could have been you but I marched on too fast and you got lost in the kitchen. I won't give up Adair, I can't, I don't want to. Nothing has changed. We can still carry on as before if you will forget this one foolish mistake I made.'

'You are very wrong, Gideon. Something *has* changed. I got a new hair-do, a few fancy clothes, and you love Adair more than you love me. So, you know what? You can have her, with my blessings. I'm leaving you.'

'A separation maybe would be no bad thing,' he quickly said.

'No, I don't want a separation. A quickie divorce, kept out of the papers for the girls' sake.'

'That really isn't necessary. Adair never meant for us to divorce,' he told Dendre.

'Well, she's going to get more than she bargained for then, isn't she?'

'What about the children?'

'They can live with you and visit me any time they like. You can keep the New York property but I would like either this house or Fire Island.'

'Hold on, hold on! Are you sure about this?'

Dendre, who had been pacing back and forth in front of Gideon, stopped. She sat down at his feet and looked up at him. 'I am in too much pain, knowing how deeply in love you are with Adair. If I were to stay with you I would suffer even more than I am now. Your disloyalty and deceit with that fuck . . . pure cruelty. I have always been your wife and don't want to become the other woman. It really doesn't suit me. I don't think we have a choice but for me to divorce you. You want to live with Adair and I still love you enough to leave you to her. My mind is made up, so please make this parting as easy for me as you can.'

Gideon took her hands in his and raised her from the floor and himself from the chair. He hugged her and wiped the tears from her eyes. For the first time in all the years they had been together he said, 'I'm sorry.'

They walked from the fireplace to sit next to each other at the table they used to dine at when they had breakfast in their bedroom. It gave them a view of the entire port and the sea beyond.

'I want this divorce to be amicable, for us to remain friends. Do you think that's possible?' he asked.

'We'll make it possible,' she answered.

'And what about Adair?'

'Civil to each other, certainly. Friendship I can't promise. Will you settle for civil?'

'Yes, and in time maybe friendship?'

'I'll try.'

'Dendre, I don't want lawyers creating a battle ground where we're both losers here. Let's work things out simply between us and let the lawyers put it into legal jargon later.

'Because you keep the books we know how much we're worth, the inventory of all my works and their whereabouts. I will write a letter and fax it to our lawyer telling him we are splitting all our assets down the middle. You are to get one half of everything we own.'

Dendre was about to say that it was very generous of him but managed to hold back. She did, after all, deserve that generosity. From the drawer Gideon pulled a pad and pencil and wrote down a few lines.

'So that takes care of that. Can I leave you to take care of the details?'

'Yes,' she told him.

'Now, the houses. I will buy you any residence you like in New York or anywhere else you want to go because I'm keeping the apartment we have there. Do you think that's fair?'

Did he expect a compliment, a thank you? True, he was giving her more than she'd ever expected. She had never even considered a settlement. How very much in love he must be, the exactness of it, the fairness, so that he did not have to linger over such things and lose time in seizing his new life with Adair. It was all happening so fast Dendre's head was spinning. She was feeling strange, in control but unaccustomed to having so much power over Gideon.

He took her silence for assent. On a piece of paper he wrote 'Hydra', on another 'Fire Island', and handed them both to Dendre. 'Neither one of us wants to give up our cherished houses so let fate choose for us. Shuffle these from hand to hand and when you're ready I will choose one. The other will be yours.'

As he unfolded his piece of paper Dendre suddenly lost her nerve. She wanted to grab it from his hand and tear into small pieces; scream, 'You bastard! Just give her up and we needn't go through all this.'

It was as if he were reading her mind; there was only one more fold. He hesitated, looked at her affectionately. He smiled at her wanly then glanced away from her at the piece of paper in his hand. 'Fire Island,' he read aloud.

It was the house she'd wanted. Dendre looked at Gideon and said, 'I'll explain to the girls and the staff.'

'I'll tell Haver. Dendre, once more, will you settle for a legal separation and stay married to me?'

'No, I think not.'

'We will speak. Any problem or question, you will call me?'

'Of course. You're my best friend, Gideon.'

'I'm happy you feel that way,' he told her as he rose to leave the room. It was an awkward moment. Neither of them knew what to do or say next.

'Just go, Gideon, there really is nothing more to say.'

'Yes, I think there is. Will it offend you if I stay in touch with Herschel, Frieda and Orlando?'

'No. As long as you don't flaunt Adair in front of them. That would offend them and hurt me. You know how much they love and respect you, so you must promise me never to take that away from them.'

'I wish you would reconsider, and settle for a separation.'

'My mind is made up, Gideon.'

'Then will you break the news to your parents, and tell them I will be in touch with them?'

Too close to tears to say another word to him, Dendre simply nodded her head.

He left the room, and Dendre went once more to the fireplace. She threw several logs on the fire and sat on the chaise watching the wood catch and the flames grow bright. She was feeling such pain, loss, numbed by what Gideon had done to her and the action she had taken. She was distracted from her feelings for a moment by the flashing light on the telephone. The studio light. She sat mesmerised by it for a long time. Gideon was on the telephone to Adair with his good news. Now, Adair, *you* will know the pain that goes with being married to him, she thought vengefully.

Dendre looked at her watch. If she hurried she could make

the last boat of the day to Athens. She quickly changed into her leather trouser suit, found her handbag and checked that her credit cards and cheque book were there. She opened the drawer where they kept cash and took half of it. There was no need to pack anything, the house was hers. When she left the room she could not help but notice the light on the telephone still flashing. She fled from the bedroom to the kitchen and found Yukio. 'I have to go to New York. I'll call you from the city and explain things.'

'I'll see you to the boat, but we'll have to hurry. Only one question, Dendre. Are the children all right?' he asked.

'Fine,' she told him, and the two of them fled from the house down the narrow cobblestone lanes.

Chapter 14

On arrival in New York, Dendre went directly to the apartment. It was in darkness and no one else was there. She turned on every light as she walked through the rooms. In her bedroom, she sat down and cried. It took her a long time before she was able to stop and when she had herself under a semblance of control she called California and woke Orlando.

'I'm divorcing Gideon,' she blurted out.

'Are you all right? Able to handle this? Oh, my dear girl, I never thought he would do this to you.'

She had been about to burst into tears, then her anger returned and she felt strong as steel. 'No, Orlando, you've got it wrong, *I've* left Gideon. It is I who has asked for a divorce.'

'Why, for heaven's sake?'

'It's actually too sordid to talk about, but the upshot of it is I'm divorcing him so I can get him back on *my* terms. You told me I was more obsessive than truly in love with Gideon. You were right about being obsessive but wrong about the love bit. I am in love with Gideon and always will be. And he – well, he doesn't realise how much he loves me. You can consider this a strategic withdrawal. I lost the battle but I intend to win the war.'

'Dendre, can't you patch it up?'

'There is nothing to patch, this divorce is amicable. I get

half of everything and he leaves all the details to me to handle.'

'Do you want me to come to New York?'

'Not for the moment.'

'Get a good lawyer. Call me as often as you like, any time you're feeling blue.'

They spoke for several minutes more and when she put down the telephone she realised that all she had said to her brother was true. She had better stop feeling blue, sorry for herself, and get on with her life.

In California, Orlando sat up in bed and thought about Dendre's call and the sad news that he had anticipated for such a long time. He loved and admired his sister for her courage, the certainty of her love for Gideon, which enabled her to take such a drastic step. He turned to look at his sleeping friend and kissed him gently on the lips, stroking the back of his hand down his lover's cheek. Until that moment, he had not realised that, like his sister, he wanted to reveal his true self, come out of the closet for all the world to see.

Dendre went to the kitchen to make herself a cup of tea. About to pour it, she went cold and shivery. The kettle still in her hand, she could think of nothing save that a ghost was walking over her grave. Dendre dropped the kettle and jumped back to avoid the boiling water that seemed to be flying everywhere. She mopped the floor and the table. Aloud she said, 'That was Adair,' and began to laugh.

Dendre picked up the pieces of broken cup that had been shattered when the kettle struck it as it hit the table. It quite frightened her, she had never before broken a dish. She sat down and looked around the kitchen, her domain, the place from which she had run her husband's and children's lives, and a life of her own which she had loved. It was over. She felt like a stranger in her own home now. Well, if not a stranger she would in future be a guest. That realisation brought her to her feet. She couldn't stay here. She picked up the telephone and called several hotels in the city. All their rooms were booked.

She was thinking where else she should call, because she had no intention of spending one night in what would soon be Adair's home, when the shrilling of the telephone broke the silence. She let it ring several times before she picked it up. It was Gideon.

'I wanted to make certain you'd arrived safely. It's strange your not being here. It was a vile thing, what I did to you, inexcusable. You didn't deserve that.'

'No, you're quite right, I didn't. Don't let's talk about it, Gideon. Let time heal that wound while we get on with our lives. I won't be staying here, I'm going to a hotel until I find an apartment.'

'Which hotel?'

'I don't know. So far the ones I've called are all booked up.'

'Fax me once you've found somewhere.'

'Gideon, would you mind if I took Yukio? There's so much to do and I'm sure Adair would prefer to have staff she can train herself.'

There was a moment of silence and then he said, 'Of course, I hadn't thought of that. I'm sure you are right. Have you called the children yet?'

'No, I intend to do that in the morning.'

'Then I can leave everything to you?'

'Yes, I told you so when we parted.'

'Goodbye,' said Gideon, and Dendre hung up the telephone.

She sat back in her chair and smiled. She knew him better than anyone else in the world. Aloud she said to the empty room, 'I give Adair a year, eighteen months at the most, then I'll be back here to stay.'

It then occurred to her that she had been penny pinching in her choice of hotel, and what for when she was a wealthy woman? She could afford any hotel she wanted. She remembered what Yukio always told her: 'Name drop first then ask for what you want.'

She called the Sherry Netherland, and for the first time in all her married years to Gideon used her name to gain an advantage. 'Hello,' she said to the switchboard, 'my name is Mrs Gideon Palenberg. May I speak to the manager?'

Dendre knew from years of experience that Gideon would not get involved with anything as mundane as explaining to the staff what had happened. So she called the Hydra house, next feeling she owed Yukio and Kitty an explanation for her sudden disappearance.

It was Kitty who answered the telephone.

'Are you all right?' she asked.

Dendre closed her eyes and sighed. She was irritated with that question. Did people think she was going to lie down and die because she had walked out on her marriage? No, of course she wasn't all right but she wasn't going to die either. Dendre ignored the question and asked Kitty if Yukio was there.

'He's just walked in,' her faithful helper told her.

'Fine, tell him to stand by, I want a word with him too.'

Dendre's mind was racing, her will kept it from fragmenting. From somewhere deep within her, she found enough strength to follow her instincts. She made a vow to focus on her objective and do whatever she had to do to achieve it.

Dendre could hear her talking to Yukio. Then she was back on the line. 'I'm here,' she said.

'Kitty, I'm not coming back to Hydra. Gideon and I have come to an amicable agreement – I am suing him for divorce.

Now, I want you to do something for me. I want you to stay on with him and take care of him. Do your job as you always have done it, but without me. When Adair has moved in with Gideon, which she will, if you are happy to be working for her, fine. If not, I want you to come work for me. The door is always open for you wherever I am. Will you do that?'

Dendre could hear her crying but finally Kitty did agree to do as she was asked.

Yukio was next on the line. She told him of the pending divorce and asked him to come to her as soon as possible. He was more controlled, asked no questions and said that Gideon had only a few minutes ago told him to leave for New York, nothing else. Dendre gave him the address where she would be. She asked for Kitty to be put on the line again and told her how grateful she had always been for everything the housekeeper had done for her and the family. That she was certain it would only be a matter of months before they would be working together again. Reassured, Kitty thanked her for being so honest with her and said that she would stay with Gideon until Adair was able to take over.

Dendre was more disturbed by the conversation than she'd thought she would be. Kitty and Yukio had been through a great deal with her. They had seen other women come and go but nothing had shaken the Palenbergs' marriage. Until Adair.

It was eight o'clock and Dendre suddenly felt pangs of hunger. She rose from her chair, gave a great sigh and went to her bedroom to pack a few things. From there she let herself into Gideon's studio and turned on the lights. Monumental beauty, passion, the essence of life jumped out of the darkness. She walked slowly down the spiral staircase, reluctant to take her eyes off the paintings, the bed with its fur cover, the brushes, the racks of pots and tubes of colour, the naked canvasses waiting for the touch of the master. She filled her lungs with the aroma of linseed oil and turpentine. Tears rolled slowly down her face and she sunk to her knees and begged God to give her strength. She had no idea how long she had been there when finally the tears dried up and she rose and left the studio.

Carrying a shoulder bag and a small case with a few things in it, she was just about to close the door to the apartment when she heard the telephone ringing. She very nearly went back inside. She had even taken a step towards doing so before she said, 'Oh, fuck it,' and slammed the door shut and double locked it. In the cab on the way to the Sherry Netherland she felt disorientated. She had never stayed in a hotel by herself. She had never stayed in such a grand place. What would Gideon say? 'You haven't done badly for a little Jewish girl from Brooklyn.' And he would have been right.

The unanswered call had been from Adair. She slammed the phone down in a temper, desperate to talk to Dendre about what had happened. To tell her herself that she was leaving for Hydra in a few days to move in with Gideon. The call would really be to try and create some sort of dialogue with Dendre where they might be friendly acquaintances, if not friends, for Gideon's sake.

Her temper ebbed quickly. She was really too happy to be angry. At last, an end to hiding their love for each other. She and Gideon could now walk hand in hand, kiss, go out as a normal couple in love. Adair had never realised how much she had wanted to be *the* woman in his life before Gideon told her Dendre and he were divorcing. To sleep the night through with him – sheer bliss! He was now at the peak of his career and she intended for him to rise higher even than that.

She hugged herself, she felt so joyful. Adair had never

really believed Dendre would leave Gideon. Now they were free *she* would be the woman he needed, had yearned for.

And what of Dendre? She would slip back to Brooklyn probably, maybe go to Florida to be near her parents, or Los Angeles to work in her brother's clinic, go with him to some third-world country with his international team of surgeons who treated the needy.

Or maybe not. Adair was certain Gideon would have settled a decent monthly allowance on her. If she lived that penny pinching life she loved so much, she need not even look for a job, just stay home and tend her garden. As for the girls . . . Well, she did have to admit they were terrifically good fun and adored Gideon and herself. They loved their mother, of course, but there would be no fun living with her. Adair would keep her own apartment and she and Gideon would live between his and her homes. The girls would be tolerated in his apartment, so long as they did not intrude.

All these things kept going through her mind. Well, I did tell Dendre not to leave him, she thought. Now he's mine, on my terms. I did warn her that trying to get rid of me would backfire and it sure has! She wondered how long she would have to stay in Hydra. Though she loved the island she was easily bored there. She needed cities like New York, Paris, London, Rome, Florence, great museums, art world pundits and scholars, dealers who revered her and her opinions. How wonderful, that Gideon and she could now travel to those places together.

When the telephone rang she ran to it, believing it was him. They were so desperate to be together without Dendre hovering in the background that they had been calling each other all day long. Adair was mad with lust for Gideon. No man before had ever been able to exploit that side of her nature to such an extent that sex was always in the forefront of her mind. They wanted each other so badly in that particular way that it was constant torment. Gideon had seduced her and held her to him in lust and love, and now they were free to tell the world about it.

She was sorely disappointed when she heard Haver's voice. She would call Gideon the moment he got off the line, she decided. She had no time even to say hello before she heard Haver talking.

'Congratulations! You must be one of the happiest women in the world right now.'

'Well, I hadn't measured my joy in quite that way but I suppose I am.'

'You've got to help me, Adair.'

'Of course, anything. All favours granted today. The Brooklyn Queen is dead, long live the Queen! Oh, dear, a bit bitchy but she did actually hand him to me.'

'You can't imagine what Gideon has done! He's given half of everything he owns to her as a divorce settlement, and that includes all his paintings and other works of art.'

Adair gasped then shouted, 'What!' She composed herself and in an icy calm voice said, 'That is simply not possible. It's like handing her a live bomb. That many Palenbergs in Dendre's hands? It is complete madness.'

'Precisely, and that's why you have to talk Gideon out of it. The money doesn't matter, but the paintings do. What if she held a revenge sale, flooded the market with them? It would badly devalue his work. She knows that and is just stupid enough to go right ahead. I know her very well. Great wealth means little or nothing to Dendre. She's in her element when she's pinching pennies. As long as I've known her there was only one thing she ever did right and that was loving Gideon. Now she doesn't even have that.'

'She'll ruin him!'

'Not if I can help it.'

'What are you going to do?' asked Adair.

'Go and see her and make her give me control of all his works. Then call Orlando. If I win him over, and I believe I can, she may listen to what he says. But, of course, before I make any such move I must see her. Gideon said he would fax me where she's staying as soon as he has word from her.'

'Nothing has been signed, has it?'

'Yes, they drew up an agreement, dictated and signed by him.'

'Oh, damn! She really held him for ransom, didn't she? He fell for it, gave her everything she asked for, he was so anxious to be rid of her.'

'Well, not quite. The way he tells it she asked for nothing, he merely offered what he thought was fair. Hang on, there's a fax coming through.'

When he returned to the telephone he told Adair, 'It's from Gideon. I'll read it to you. "Dendre living in the Sherry Netherland".'

For several seconds neither of them spoke. 'I'd have thought the Chelsea Hotel would have been more to her liking. This is very out of character,' said Haver in a worried voice.

'So were the other things: her attempts at glamourising her looks, for instance. She even made a call on me here demanding I leave Gideon or else. I think we may have underestimated Dendre. I'll do what I can with Gideon. You'd better go see her before that bomb goes off.'

Dendre went directly to the receptionist's desk and gave her name. Though the receptionist was being discreet, she caught him looking her over. When he smiled it was as if she had passed inspection as the wife of a great man. Dendre was amused by the incident. He handed the key to the porter who

193

was standing by with her shabby shoulder bag and small case. The manager appeared to greet her and welcome her to the hotel. She looked around the quiet lobby with its antique furnishings and sumptuous flower arrangements. The thick carpet felt luxurious under her feet. There was an atmosphere of quiet elegance. Nothing shouted at you. It seemed more like a gentlemen's club than a hotel.

'Will Mr Palenberg be joining you?' asked the manager with a hopeful look in his eye.

'No, I think not.'

The lift shot up through the building with the manager and Dendre discussing the weather. He saw her into her suite. The small sitting room was charming, a little too grand for her taste but she could appreciate it for what it was. The manager asked a porter to please light the fire.

He showed Dendre the view over Central Park from a glass turret with a buttoned banquette scattered with cushions. Only the hotel's very best rooms had them. There was something elegant but homely about the suite. From the reception room, Mr Dobson led her through to a small pantry completely equipped, and then into a large bedroom. The furniture in the room was handsome, an early American mahogany four-poster bed and chest of drawers. Throughout the suite the walls were a deep cream colour, the fabrics were in shades of white with textures from silk damask to linen, the draperies in different shades of white and cream and tarnished silver, the floors were wooden with oriental carpets covering them. There were marvellous fresh flowers everywhere: tulips, sprays of baby orchids, daffodils, and several varieties of lilies including the pure white Casablanca lily. The flowers gave the accent of colour in each room. It was as if the suite had been decorated as a background for them. The bathroom was peach and white marble and the taps were sterling silver.

'Will this do, Mrs Palenberg? It's the best I could do on such short notice.'

'Yes, but I think it must be too expensive for my budget.'

'I'll charge you the price of a single room not a suite, will that do?'

'That's very generous of you, but why would you do that?'

'Because it's an honour to have you staying with us and because it was all I could offer you.'

Dendre thanked him then spoke about Yukio. 'My assistant is arriving tomorrow or the next day. Do you have any facilities for guests' staff? He is a Japanese gentleman who has been with us for many years.'

'I dare say we can find something for him.'

After the manager left, Dendre walked round the suite. A little too grand, but comfortable and cosy was her verdict. The only thing she could fault were the paintings. She thought how marvellous the rooms would look with Gideon's painting and sculpture arranged here, the pre-Columbian works of art they'd collected over the years, the Henry Moores, Hans Hoffmans, Max Ernsts – so many things they owned.

Pangs of hunger became too serious for to her contemplate doing anything but eating. She quickly changed into a smart black dress and slipped on her full-length chinchilla coat which she had at the last minute thrown over her arm as she fled from the apartment.

In the lobby, just as she was walking towards the door, she saw Haver. She was neither disturbed nor annoyed to see him. Accepting would be more like it. That was new and different for Dendre since she had never been fully at ease before with him. The day they had met and he had given her his painter's wife speech she had accepted his terms of

195

no interference. They'd had remarkably little to do with one another since then.

Haver had not as yet become accustomed to the new glamorous Dendre. He was taken aback at first by seeing her looking so smart, especially in the lobby of the Sherry Netherland.

'You're going out? I was hoping to have a word with you.'

'I take it Gideon faxed you with my address? I do know it's essential I talk to you, Haver, but frankly I'm too hungry to think of anything but food right now. So I'll call you tomorrow.'

'No! I'll take you to dinner,' he offered.

'Are you sure?' she asked.

'Yes, positively.'

'That's nice of you. Somewhere not too far.'

'How about the Oak Room at the Plaza? It's only across the street.'

As they entered the Oak Room it struck Dendre how remarkable it was that whenever she and Gideon had gone out on the spur of the moment with Haver, he always got a table. After they had been seated at a very good one she naively asked him how he managed it.

'My dear, it's very easy. I am a *very, very* big tipper. An obscenely big tipper. That's what it takes to get what you want in this city.'

Haver was appalled when she asked for bread and butter with her glass of champagne. He told the waiter, 'Fresh *fois gras* and toast and butter, and a bottle of your best Sauternes to go with the *fois gras*. And do please hurry, we're famished.'

'Not even a pretzel while we wait for the *pâté*?'

He signalled for a waiter and seconds later there was a bowl of salted almonds on the table. After eating several Dendre told him, 'That's better. I expect you and Adair have been crowing over my setting Gideon free?'

Haver looked embarrassed as he told her, 'Not exactly. We're more concerned for you both now that you have asked for a divorce. Look, is this too painful to talk about?'

'Oh, it's painful but I have to get used to it. There are so many other people involved. I haven't even called the girls yet.'

'Whyever did you do it, Dendre? Why couldn't you have left things as they were? You can still patch it up.'

'How? Shoot Adair? He won't, so I will, one way or another. I left him because he loves her more than he loves me, or so he thinks. It's as simple as that. In all the years I have been married to Gideon I was never the other woman. His love for Adair is so strong that he was making me into that. I'd rather be the wife than the mistress any day. Finally, I had no choice. Now can we please drop the whys and wherefores? Subject closed.'

The *fois gras* was washed down with the perfect sweetness of the Sauternes. It was over pheasant in cream, Calvados and apples, served with crisp *rosti* and red cabbage, that he casually, much too casually, said, 'I want to be honest with you, Dendre. I think Gideon has made an enormous mistake in giving you half his work as your settlement. I intend to try and change his mind about that. It's very bad business to split a collection.'

She was astounded that he should try to interfere in her private affairs, business or no business. She put her knife and fork down and looked across the table at him. 'And what did Gideon say?'

'That he had given you what he thought was a fair settlement, and if I wanted to say anything about what was now your collection, I should say it to you.'

'Did he add anything else?'

'Yes. When I said it was irresponsible of him to have made such a move as that without consulting me, that handing you half his collection was like handing you a ticking bomb, he laughed and replied, "You never did understand her, Haver. Always underestimated her."'

Since Dendre had walked out on Gideon, she had not given one thought to what she was going to do with one of the world's greatest private collections of a living artist. She had hardly an idea about anything beyond calling the girls, her parents and her lawyer to hand over the paper Gideon had signed asking him to arrange a quick divorce and working with Yukio on dividing the Palenberg estate.

'Have you spoken to Adair about this?' she asked Haver.

'You know I have never lied to you and I don't intend to start now. Yes, I did, and asked her to try to intercede, persuade Gideon to make a different arrangement with you that did not break up the collection. You understand this isn't personal, just business?'

'Haver, in all the years I have known and disliked you, I could never quite understand why. Until now. You are devoid of real emotion, have no idea what true love is or how people behave once they have experienced that special feeling. I have always closed my eyes to the lack of respect you have for me – just a little short of disdain is how I would put it. The reason I did that was because your handling of Gideon's career has been absolutely brilliant, just as he said it would be. We trusted you implicitly and were right to. It never occurred to me what I would do with my settlement except to claim it and place it in a safe, secure place. I assumed you would carry on being a dealer on my behalf as you have been for Gideon.

'And then the final insult! You think I'm too stupid to own and care for Gideon's work and deal with *my* collection. That

I am such a spineless character, so bird-brained, that Gideon needs you and Adair to step in and save him from ruin. That I would be vindictive enough to get back at him through the most important thing in his life: his work. I never envisaged anyone else, including myself, being Gideon's dealer except you. Until now.'

She threw her napkin on the table and rose from her chair. Haver was still so traumatised by this new, assertive Dendre, and having lost half the Palenberg collection, he remained silent.

'In deference to Gideon's generosity, I will, when I think it necessary, consult you on any moves I make that might affect the market for Palenbergs.

'I don't think there will be any need for us to see each other for some time, since I have records of the entire collection and the whereabouts of each item up to date on my computer. You must feel free to call me if you have a problem. I'll send you a copy of my inventory and the whereabouts of my pieces. If you ever want to talk business, feel free to call me.'

Without another word she walked away from the table. Haver sat down, dazed. Suddenly she was back at the table again. Once more he rose from his chair. He looked shattered, as well he might. Haver Savage had probably made the greatest single mistake of his career.

'Feel like a fool, Haver. You should! Greed and the need to control, desperation to win or at the very least hold all the cards to your chest, just did you in. But that's not what I came back to say. It was to ask you to pass on a message to Adair.

'Gideon will love me again and more than she will be able to bear. Tell her I give her a year at the most.'

Chapter 15

Twelve months was not a long time to do all the things Dendre had to do to win Gideon back on her own terms. Eight months had passed and she was still living in her suite of rooms at the Sherry Netherland. The one thing she had realised as she'd fled from the Plaza and her dinner partner was that the art sharks were going to come after her as soon as word was out that she now controlled one of the largest private collections of Palenbergs. They would all be circling her in a feeding frenzy.

She knew she was vulnerable. Had observed over the years other painters' wives and how they had been used and abused by some of the more ruthless dealers and museums, promising them a special wing or a room with a plaque honouring them for their donations. Most of those donations then remained in the museum's vaults for lack of the space that had been promised.

Instinct had told her two things that night eight months before: she would have to move faster than the sharks and keep herself focused on her return to Gideon. It had been during her first night at the Sherry that she realised there would be no time to find a flat and decorate it if she was to achieve everything else she planned.

Now she was lying in bed watching television with Pieta and Daisy fast asleep on either side of her. It was late and she would have to wake them because Gideon and Adair were picking them up to take them to an exhibition and dinner.

Dendre never saw Gideon with Adair. They had tried that several times and it had upset Adair too much. She resented the fact that she had no control over him when it came to his children or his former wife. Of course there was another reason why she was disturbed by Dendre's presence: she knew that Dendre intended to win him back.

Sitting in the taxi waiting for Gideon to return with the girls, Adair tried to work out why she was so unhappy. She seemed always to be making the wrong choices, never getting what she really wanted. She tried to analyse what was going wrong between Gideon and herself and thought back to that wonderful euphoric day when she had arrived in Hydra. Gideon had met her at the boat and swept her up in his arms, whispering in her ear how much he loved her. The Hydriots standing around them clapped their hands, laughed and teased him.

Gideon had taken her directly to the bedroom where he had undressed her and himself and they had had sex. In all the sex they had had together previously, he had never been such a free spirit. It only added to his attraction for Adair. He was more like a thirty-year-old than a man of his age and he captured her heart all over again. After four days alone with him, making love and lust the priority of their lives, she had realised she never wanted to live without Gideon. She now wanted to marry him, something she had always denied before.

One day they sailed to a deserted island and scrambled over the rocks. It was gloriously sunny and warm for that time of year. Gideon ordered her to take off her clothes. He watched as she undressed, enjoying enormously what he saw and how submissive she had become. He was besotted with her because he was able to bring her body to submission but never her mind. He had enormous respect for his lover and what she had done with her life. Adair knew that. It was one of the reasons she loved him.

It was strange to be thinking of that rock and what had happened there, sitting in a taxi in a New York City downpour. But it was still so vivid to her. Gideon had tied her hands with her scarf and ordered her to lie down on the rock. A wind had quite suddenly blown up but that only added to the excitement of the moment. Gideon covered her with his body, teased her with his erect penis by sliding it between her vaginal lips. She was in a frenzy and begged him to take her. He entered her as she asked but had done no more. Again she had to beg him to fuck her until he did. The wind was stronger now, frighteningly so. Adair came. She screamed into the wind and came again and again. He pulled her up off the rock and into his arms. The wind whipped her hair. She looked wild, untamed. She wrapped her legs around his waist and, consumed by lust, he ordered her to separate her vaginal lips and impale herself upon him. It was she now who with unbound hands on his waist was doing the fucking. But not for long. Multiple orgasms took her over. Gideon, having worn her out, once more took control.

The taxi driver broke into her memories and asked how long they were going to be. She answered just a few more minutes. Looking through the door to the hotel she could see Gideon had not gone up to Dendre's room. In her thoughts she returned to that afternoon on the rock. It was one of the most important days of her life because at that moment, when they came together, he shouted to her over the wind, 'Adair, will you marry me the day I receive my divorce?' and she had shouted back, 'Oh, yes, please.'

They were married ten days later in the American Embassy in Athens.

'Better open the door, here comes your husband and the ladies.'

The doorman popped open his umbrella and the girls huddled under it. Gideon was already walking bare-headed in the heavy rain towards her. Seeing them made something snap in Adair's head. *That* was what was making her so unhappy. She detested family life. Domesticity and Gideon's love for it had turned her into a second Dendre in eight short months. Adair felt she was going to be sick. How had she allowed herself to slide into this trap? Well, I'll have to do something about it, she vowed to herself.

The reason it had taken so long for Gideon and the girls to get down to the lobby was because he had had a long conversation on the house telephone with Dendre. When she hung up, she told her daughters, 'Your father is waiting in the lobby for you.'

'He talked to you for a long time, Mom. I think he still loves you. What do you think?' asked Pieta.

'That he still loves me,' she confirmed.

'His life is a mess without you,' said Daisy.

'I know that too.'

'Adair does try but she hates giving herself up to running Dad's life. She can't cook, and wants to eat out all the time,' said Daisy.

'Hey, we all agreed – no telling tales.'

'Oh, Mom.' Then Daisy stopped short. When Dendre had told the girls about the divorce they took it very well because she had promised to explain it all to them in time. That for now it was essential they stay out of any dispute and enjoy Adair as they always had.

It had been Amber who had said to the other girls at that time, 'Let's not cause any problems. If I know Mom and Dad like I think I do, some day we will all be back under the same roof.'

'Just think what Amber said,' Dendre reminded them, 'and let's all get on with living one day at a time. OK, girls, Dad and Adair are waiting.' And she kissed them goodbye.

For all his fame and fortune, Gideon and his family had always remained aloof enough to remain very private people, not gossiped about in the tabloid press or glossy magazines. Gideon lived in an elitist society, and even within that society was rarely seen. His divorce and remarriage to Adair was talked about in only a very small circle of people, and only a very few of them were privy to the details of what Gideon had settled on her upon the divorce.

Dendre had been working at the speed of lightning on her new life. There was a truce of sorts with Haver because as much as he detested talking to a mere painter's wife about business, here was one case where he was obliged to. For all that, no matter how clever he was with Dendre, he had never been able to wheedle anything out of her about what she was doing with her collection or even where it was.

Only her two lovers, Ben Borgnine and Talbot Lee, a well-known and respected sculptor, knew what she was doing. But the day was drawing near when the entire art world would be talking about Dendre's decision. She felt very strongly that Gideon should be told by her before the press got hold of it. That had been why, when he had been talking on the hotel telephone with her, she had asked if he might take her to lunch one day soon and give her some time afterwards. They had made a date for the following day.

Now, as she was bathing, she thought about this new life she had been living for the last eight months, the good and the bad things that had happened to her. The worst thing was the pain of not being with Gideon. Not a day went by when she didn't want to be his wife, his lover, his friend. What had eased that pain had been the fun of flirting with all the eligible men who suddenly found her irresistible once they found out about her divorce settlement. Men in the art and other worlds who had in the past ignored her as a dull wife and kitchen drudge, now wooed her, begged to bed her. She played with them as a cat plays with a mouse, clever gigolos included. A single woman multi-millionaire, on the loose and reputedly vulnerable . . . ambitious male escorts were soon calling her by the dozen. They were so blatant, she was more embarrassed for them than she was for herself. Why did she even bother to go out with them? There was an easy answer: Adair. Part of Dendre's campaign to rid herself of Adair was to show her rival that she was not the simple woman Adair had been so eager to dismiss her as. 'The mouse that roared' she had called Dendre right to her face. Well, this mouse intended to deafen Adair.

Of all the men Dendre had gone out with, she was only sleeping with Ben and Talbot. The two men knew about this but never treated each other as rivals in love. They both knew they were no more than friends and temporary sexual partners to Dendre and could never be anything more because she intended to go back to Gideon.

Not that either of them ever spoke to her or to each other about that. There was something about the way she made love. It was erotic, thrilling sex. Both men considered her sexuality as something special. Her wild, adventurous soul shone in the bedroom. Gideon had the reputation of being an extraordinary lover, his former wife only a submissive creature, a door mat for him to wipe his feet on. How wrong the gossips had been!

Yukio tapped at the bathroom door and announced that Mr Talbot was waiting for her in the drawing room. Dendre was late and disliked being so. She all but jumped from the bath. Slipping into a terrycloth robe, she went through her bedroom to the door leading to the drawing room, opened it a crack and saw Talbot holding a glass of straight malt whisky in his hand. He was looking very handsome: tall and lean with a head of dark blond hair and a beard cut short. His dark blue eyes were frank and sexy, telling all about his character.

He was wearing a leather jacket and buff-coloured corduroy trousers, just the look to suit his character. He was contemplating one of Gideon's paintings. Dendre had had all the hotel's removed and had replaced them with Palenbergs. The suite now contained many wonderful things she had taken possession of in her settlement. These works of art had changed the bland hotel rooms into grand salons housing several million dollars worth of art treasures.

There was something carnal about Talbot, a kind of chemistry she found irresistible. Dendre opened the door and beckoned him into the bedroom. He smiled and then laughed.

'You have become shameless – thank God,' he told her as he held his glass to her lips.

Dendre sipped the malt whisky. The smoky taste warmed her. Almost immediately she wanted more. Talbot sat on the bed and she left the room to get another glass and bring the decanter to the bedroom. When she returned he had turned down the bed cover, removed his clothes and climbed into bed. She handed him the bottle and the glass and went round the room picking up his clothes.

'At least Gideon picked up after himself.'

Talbot watched her as she moved around. 'Any other complaints, madam?'

'No, I don't think so,' she answered as she removed her robe and slipped into bed next to him.

Talbot placed an arm around her and she leaned against him. 'Well, what news do you have? What have you been doing?' he asked as he caressed her breasts.

One of the things she liked most about having sex with him was that they were like old friends. They would always tell each other what they had been doing since the last time they'd met. He would discuss his work, she would tell him what progress she had made with the project she was working on. They enjoyed their pillow talk but gradually it tapered off as their caresses, kisses and hunger for something more carnal became overwhelming.

Tonight Talbot made love to Dendre rather than just had sex. It was unlike anything they had been having for the few months since they had been seeing each other. They sated their lust and after bathing together went back to bed.

'What happened to us tonight?' asked Dendre. 'And don't tell me we had sex, I know that.'

'A serious, unexpected problem has arisen. We're falling in love. Love governed that fuck,' he said, a note of sadness in his voice.

Dendre knew he was right. She had never had sex like that except for the last time she'd had sex with Gideon in Hydra, and left him. What Talbot had said was true, they did have a serious problem. The last thing she wanted was to complicate her already complicated life with a love affair in which she could only be dishonest.

'I know,' she said.

He sat up and took her in his arms. 'Love will never work for us. You know why, let's not discuss it. I think we have to nip this in the bud before it blossoms, you lose your focus and I get hurt. Better to remain friends, loving friends, don't you think?'

'Yes. But I will miss you enormously.'

'Oh, dear, silly Dendre, friends don't desert friends, not even for a love that cannot be. We'll just have to give up sex with one another and find partners we can love and fuck at the same time.'

'Talbot . . .'

'No, let's not talk about it. Just revel in our last night in bed together.'

When Dendre awakened in the morning Talbot was gone. She fell back on the pillows and thought about what had happened between them. Talbot and she had been right to part as lovers but remain devoted friends. She was grateful the affair had ended in such a romantic and honourable way. But that first fling after the divorce, so filled with passion, had taught her one thing: sex without love was not for her. She wanted from Gideon what they had once had together before Adair came into the picture, love *and* sex, and she was determined to have it with him again or give up her quest to return to him.

There was a knock at her bedroom door. It was Yukio. She slipped into a dressing gown and back into bed then told him to come in. He did, bearing a mass of long-stemmed white roses. The card read:

I will always think of you as my most splendid lady.
Yours, Talbot

She looked at the roses, held them close to her face and breathed in their perfume. Then she handed them to Yukio, saying, 'Put them in the pantry and get out our most beautiful vase, I want to arrange these myself. Have you had breakfast?

I'm going to make scrambled eggs and toast. Shall I make it for two?'

'Yes, please,' answered Yukio, who sensed something had happened to get Dendre back in the kitchen. She had hardly gone into the pantry to cook anything in all the eight months they had been living here. Everything had been sent up from the Sherry Netherland or they had settled for Chinese take-away.

Dendre was dressing for her meeting with Gideon when the telephone rang. It was her father calling from Florida. There was nothing unusual about that; her parents' calls were as frequent as they had always been when she was married to Gideon. They had been marvellous about her divorcing Gideon, especially as divorce was absolutely unacceptable to them. She credited their behaviour with the fact that they knew she had left Gideon so that they could come back together in a better marriage than before.

Frieda had cried and asked, 'What will I tell my neighbours, family, friends?'

Her father had been listening on the bedroom extension. He had answered for Dendre. 'Tell them nothing, Frieda. Think of this sad event as a chess game that Dendre is playing. And you know our Dendre, she never plays a game unless she's got more than a fifty per cent chance of winning.'

'This is crazy! My daughter is in the middle of the worst tragedy in her life and you tell me to think of it as a chess game! Is that what will win her husband back, I ask you?'

'Yes,' both Herschel and Dendre had replied.

There had been a long moment of silence from Frieda before she announced, 'So be it. I never did understand chess. So I won't ask any more questions. Just let me know when you've won the game.'

And, to their credit, neither her mother nor her father asked what was happening between her and Gideon. Herschel opened their telephone conversation now as he always did. 'So what's happening? Are you and the girls all right?'

'The girls are just fine. I'm very well, just dressing to go out to lunch with Gideon.'

'Is that good news or bad?' asked her father.

Until he had asked the question, Dendre had not thought whether it was good or bad in relation to what she was about to do. But now he had made her think about it, she realised that it was profoundly good.

'Good news, Dad.'

'You mean you've got the king on the run, or is it check mate?' asked Herschel.

'I'll call you tonight and tell you. The game isn't over yet.'

'I wish I were a betting man.'

Dendre laughed. 'Well, who would you put your money on if you were such a man?'

'Well, it wouldn't be Adair.'

'Dad, I love you.'

'I love you too.'

On that note they said goodbye.

Gideon arrived at her rooms at one o'clock. Yukio let him in and Gideon said, 'I certainly miss you and Kitty. My home life's a mess.'

'I suppose it would be cruel to say I'm not surprised, Gideon. Adair is a lot of things but I don't think she appreciates domesticity,' replied Yukio.

Gideon laughed. 'No, she doesn't understand home and hearth.'

Dendre had heard all this from the bedroom where the door stood open. She took one last look in the mirror then went to greet her ex-husband.

She had chosen her clothes carefully: black suede min
skirt and pre-Columbian gold jewellery. Pieces that Gideon
had bought for her; reminders, she hoped, of the many
wonderful years they'd had together. For the first time since
they had been divorced Dendre saw a look in his eyes and a
smile on his lips that were both loving and carnal.

'For a naive little girl from Brooklyn, you've come a long
way. You look so stunningly smart! Still a woman without
labels, still a woman who can surprise me,' he teased.

'Why is it that when I'm with you, I always feel like that
woman from Brooklyn who married Gideon Palenberg? It's
such a comfortable feeling so, you see, you don't have to
remind me, Gideon,' she said sweetly.

'I've missed you since the day you left me. I've wanted
to tell you that a thousand times.' And he started to walk
towards her.

Gideon loved her. She had always known that, and so had
he. Dendre's heart was bursting with joy. He took her in his
arms and kissed her on the lips. The kiss was not erotic but
full of love and tenderness and yearning for her. He held her
in his arms, gazed into her eyes, then stepped back and told
her, 'I never appreciated how much I love you.'

'Yes, you did, but you never wanted to admit it to yourself.
Please, Gideon, let's not talk about the past. And before you
say any more, let me tell you several things I would not want
you to hear from anyone else. Let's do it over lunch, in a more
public place where I can keep my nerve.'

Gideon felt sick with fear. He had never had that feeling
before. He realised he loved Dendre and the pain of that love
struck him like a blow. He followed her from her suite and
out of the hotel, dazed by his feelings. He could wait no
longer. As the doorman opened the taxi door, Gideon pulled
her aside.

'I love you, Dendre, more than any other woman. You're my world – I need you, want you. We'll begin again. Please marry me again? A corner of my life has been empty since you left and Adair has neither the love nor the inclination to fill it.'

'Can I answer you after we have had lunch?' she told him, her heart pounding, tears of joy brimming in her eyes.

The doorman and the taxi driver had heard it all and were touched by Gideon's declaration of love. Dendre entered the taxi and before Gideon could follow, the driver said, 'You don't often see love in the streets of New York. My guess is, she'll say yes.'

Gideon relaxed suddenly. A guess from a New York City taxi driver and all was well with his world again. In the taxi going to the Four Seasons neither Gideon nor Dendre spoke a word. Yet there was no tension in their silence. They had always been comfortable without words.

While paying the driver, who was given a huge tip, Gideon turned to Dendre and said, 'Adair talks too much, it grates on my nerves.' They burst out laughing and Dendre felt a moment of sheer bliss. Gideon was out of love with Adair! She took his hand and together they mounted the steps of the Seagram Building to go to lunch.

Gideon ordered champagne before turning to her. 'I hate this place – I find it pretentious. Not right for you or me. That was why I chose it. We won't know anyone, ergo we won't be disturbed.'

He'd no sooner finished speaking than hovering next to them was the architect Philip Johnson. Gideon jumped up and before Johnson could open his mouth said, 'Philip, I don't mean to be rude but we want to be alone.' Johnson walked off in a huff.

'He'll never forgive you for that,' said Dendre.

'So?' answered Gideon, draining his wine after touching the rim of his glass to Dendre's.

'Quite right. You've always been right about people, and the world, and me, Gideon.' Dendre couldn't help but notice how happy he was to hear that. He reached for her hand but she drew it away.

'Gideon, the reason I have asked you to take me to lunch is that I want you to know what I have been doing since we divorced. Remember when I called you and asked for the money to buy a new house and you sent it to me?'

'Yes,' he answered, looking very puzzled.

'Well, I didn't buy a new house to live in here in the city. Though I did buy a building.'

'I don't understand? I know you wouldn't take money from me for one thing then use it for another thing entirely. So what kind of a building did you buy?'

'A multi-storey car park! Please don't ask any more questions. Let me just tell you. Once I realised the enormity of the divorce settlement, and having listened to Haver talk sense about it needing to be handled properly, I began to consider my options. Haver was ruthlessly honest with me and obviously considered me too dumb to deal with what had become my collection. He showed me how greedy and unkind, ruthless and manipulative, dealers are. He opened my eyes to the art world and how it would suddenly court poor stupid Dendre Palenberg. I very quickly caught on to who were the good guys and who were the sharks. It was all rather interesting but made me more concerned than ever about my collection.

'I thought it over and came back to the one idea that seemed to work for me. The paintings were mine to do with as I wanted. Then some other factors came into it. You had given me the collection and that you did so seemed to me

214

proof of how much you still loved me. An acknowledgement of how important I was to you. That was what I so wanted from you the night you received your medal from the President.

'I talked to several museum people, who of course all wanted to have the collection, but I did not trust them to do what I wanted. Then it came to me: a private museum, open to the public by appointment only. I had intended always to let Haver deal with selling any of my collection as well as yours. That made good business sense – something with which he did not credit me. Then I told Ben Borgnine about my plan, in confidence, and he helped me. He suggested I go to several private museums in Europe and talk to the owners, which I did.

'I stole a curator from the Museum of Modern Art for my museum, and I.M. Pei to design the building. On the top floor is an apartment for me or the curator.

'Now, in answer to your proposal made so lovingly in the street, Gideon – I never really left you.'

'I always knew you were clever, but you never believed it yourself,' he told her. 'I'm astounded at what you have done, and so very happy for you. You will make an enormous impression on the art world. But you still haven't answered – will you marry me?'

'Why? To go back to the kitchen, walk behind you as no more than your shadow? I'm afraid it's too late for that. But to walk *next* to you, be loved more than you have ever loved another woman – yes, I certainly will, as soon as you're free to marry me.'